"Stay here," he whispered, and reached beneath his tuxedo jacket to pull his gun from his holster. Armed, he headed toward her bedroom.

"Be careful," she whispered back, her sweet voice trembling with concern. For him?

Her words touched something inside Whit— something that he'd closed off years ago. The part of him that had yearned to have someone—anyone— give a damn about him. Of course she didn't really care, but those words distracted him enough that when he stepped inside the bedroom, the intruder got the drop on him. Before his eyes could even adjust to the darkness, something struck his head— knocking him down and knocking him out—leaving the princess at the mercy of the intruder....

LISA CHILDS

THE PRINCESS PREDICAMENT

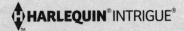
HARLEQUIN® INTRIGUE®

To Tara Gavin and Melissa Jeglinski,
with deep appreciation for your professional expertise
and your warm friendship!

ISBN-13: 978-0-373-74731-3

Recycling programs
for this product may
not exist in your area.

THE PRINCESS PREDICAMENT

Printed in U.S.A.

www.Harlequin.com

ABOUT THE AUTHOR

Bestselling, award-winning author Lisa Childs writes paranormal and contemporary romance for Harlequin Books. She lives in Michigan with her two daughters, a talkative Siamese and a long-haired Chihuahua who thinks she's a rottweiler. Lisa loves hearing from readers, who can contact her through her website, www.lisachilds.com, or snail-mail address, P.O. Box 139, Marne, MI 49435.

Books by Lisa Childs

All backlist available in ebook. Don't miss any of our special offers. Write to us at the following address for information on our newest releases.

Harlequin Reader Service
U.S.: 3010 Walden Ave., P.O. Box 1325, Buffalo, NY 14269
Canadian: P.O. Box 609, Fort Erie, Ont. L2A 5X3

CAST OF CHARACTERS

Princess Gabriella St. Pierre—The royal heiress has been in danger and betrayed—she doesn't know whom she can trust. After falling for a man who doesn't care about her, she doesn't even trust herself.

Whitaker Howell—The royal bodyguard has been assigned to keep the princess safe but winds up putting her in more danger. Whit willingly risks his life to save her but fights to keep from losing his heart, too.

Prince Linus Demetrios—The jilted fiancé kidnapped the wrong woman once—this time he's determined to get the right one.

King Octavius Demetrios—He's determined to merge his country with Princess Gabriella's—by whatever means necessary.

Prince Tonio Malamatos—The princess's current fiancé is determined to marry the princess—despite the fact she doesn't love him or even know him.

Honora Del Cachon—She's lost her fiancé to her royal cousin and is full of the fury of a woman scorned.

Zeke Rogers—The former security guard to the king is about to lose his job to Whitaker Howell and his partner—perhaps he intends a ransom to be his retirement plan.

Chapter One

Six months earlier...

"I'm going to kill him! Let me in there!"

Whit Howell had been hired as the king's bodyguard to protect him from political threats and criminals—not from his own daughter. But as furious as Princess Gabriella St. Pierre was at the moment, she posed the greatest threat Whit had encountered yet during the ten weeks he'd been on the job.

"Your royal highness," he addressed her as protocol required even though they were alone in the hallway outside the door to the king's wing of the palace. "Your father has retired for the night and will not be disturbed."

"You damn well better believe he's going to be disturbed," she said, her usually soft, sweet voice rising to a nearly hysterical shout. "He'll be lucky to be alive when I'm done with him!" She rushed toward the double mahogany doors, but Whit stepped in front of them.

She slammed into him, her breasts flattening against his chest. With her stiletto heels on, her forehead came to his chin. Her hair—a thick golden brown, was falling over the tiara on her head and into her face and rubbing against his throat.

With her face flushed and caramel-brown eyes flashing with temper, she had never been more beautiful. He doubted she would graciously accept that compliment, though, so he bit his tongue to hold it back. Of course he had noticed she was attractive before but in the kind of untouchable, one-dimensional way that a model in a magazine was attractive. She hadn't seemed real then.

She certainly hadn't acted like any woman he'd ever known. Not only was she beautiful but also sweet and gracious—even to the people her father considered servants. She had seemed more fairy-tale fantasy than reality.

She was real now. And quite touchable. She put her hands on his arms and tried to shove him aside, so she could get through the doors to her father's rooms.

While she was tall, she was slender—with not enough muscle to budge him. She let out a low growl of frustration and then fisted her hands and started pounding on his chest. "Get out of my way! Get out of my way!"

Damn. If she raised her voice any louder, she was likely to disturb the king. And Whit couldn't lose this security job. Assignments like this had been hard to come by the past three years. So he stepped closer to her, using his body to gently push her back from the door. She kept swinging even as she stumbled. So he caught her around the waist and lifted her— up high to swing her over his shoulder. Then he touched a button on the two-way radio in his ear.

"Aaron?"

"Put me down!" Princess Gabriella screamed, pounding on his back now.

He crossed the wide hall, moving farther away from the tall wood doors to the king's wing. Then he touched the button again to call his partner. Former partner. They were no longer in the security business together. They had actually been hired separately to protect the king.

It was Aaron's night off, which he'd had to postpone until after the ball that had been held earlier that evening. But usually Aaron would still be on the job; the man was always on the job.

"Aaron? Timmer?"

Maybe his partner answered but Whit couldn't hear him over the princess's shouts. Her yelling had drawn some of the other palace guards to the hall outside the king's private quarters. Whit gestured at one of the men he'd personally hired, a man with whom he'd served in Afghanistan, like he had with Aaron Timmer. He could trust him to guard King St. Pierre while he deposited the princess in her private rooms.

"Stop! Put me down!" she ordered, her tone nearly as imperious as her father's.

There was none of the sweetness and graciousness Whit had seen in her the past couple of months that he'd been guarding the king. While she had always talked to him as she did to all the *help,* with him she had seemed especially shy and nervous—nothing like the woman currently pounding on his back. The sweet woman had attracted him; the angry woman exasperated and excited him.

As he carried her past the other guard, she implored the man, "Stop him!"

Like he trusted the guard, the guard trusted Whit, a lot more than Aaron trusted him now. The guard let them pass.

"You creep!" she hurled insults as she pounded harder on his back. "You son of a bitch!" She added some even more inventive insults, using words he wouldn't have thought someone as privileged as she would even know. Then she ordered him, "Get your hands off me!"

She wriggled in his grasp, her breasts pushing against his back while her hip rubbed against his shoulder. She had curves in all the right places—curves that he wanted to touch…

But he shouldn't have been able to get his hands on her in the first place. Since the day, as an infant, she had been brought home to the palace, there had been threats to her safety. People had tried to kidnap her to ransom her for money or political influence from the king. To make sure that none of those abduction attempts were successful, she had been protected her entire life but never more so than now. Usually…

"Where the hell's *your* bodyguard?" he wondered aloud. Even though he hated the woman who protected the princess, he couldn't criticize how the former U.S. Marshal did her job. She went above and beyond to keep the young heiress safe; she had even had plastic surgery so that she looked exactly like Gabriella St. Pierre.

Could it be that they had switched places…
It made more sense that the woman he'd

slung over his shoulder was the bodyguard than the princess…because the bodyguard rarely let the princess out of her sight. Unless she had secured her in her rooms and was now masquerading as her.

For what purpose?

To attack the king?

After the announcement her father had made at the ball that evening, the princess had more reason—a damn good reason—to want to hurt the man who had so hurt and humiliated her. Whit had done the right thing to not let her into the monarch's wing of rooms. Because if she really was the princess, he could understand why she was so pissed, and he wouldn't have blamed her had she wanted to kill her own father. But he couldn't let her—or her bodyguard—complete the task.

Which woman was she?

It mattered to him. He didn't want his pulse racing like crazy over the bodyguard. He didn't want his hands tingling with the need to touch her wriggling body. He had never been attracted to the former Marshal, and he didn't want to be.

Charlotte Green had already cost him too much. Just like every other woman he'd ever had contact with, she hadn't given a damn about him. Maybe she didn't really give a damn about the princess, either.

No guard stood sentry at the entrance to the princess's suite. He pushed open the unlocked door and strode down the hall to her private rooms and found no security there either. If the princess had been left in her wing of the palace, Charlotte Green had left her unprotected. No matter how much he despised her, he doubted she would have done that. But she wouldn't have let the royal heiress go running off on her own, either.

Sure, they were *inside* the palace. But that didn't mean they were safe, especially with guests from the ball spending the night in the palace. And even if they weren't, sometimes the greatest threats to one's life were the people closest to them. The princess had learned that tonight.

She must have also learned that yelling and struggling wasn't going to compel him to release her because she'd fallen silent and still. Her body was tense against his. And warm and soft...

And entirely distracting.

He needed to deposit her in her rooms and get the hell back to his post. Using his free hand, the one not holding tight to the back of her toned thigh, he opened the door to her sitting room. Painted a bright yellow, the room was sunny and completely different from her father's darkly paneled rooms. After going inside, he released her, and she moved, sliding down his body—every curve pressing against him. He bit back a groan as desire overwhelmed him, and he was the tense one now.

As her feet touched the floor, she stepped back, and then stumbled and fell against him. He caught her shoulders in his hands to steady her, and he realized she'd lost a shoe somewhere along the route to her room. She stood before him in only one stiletto slip-on sandal. She really was a fairy-tale princess; she was freaking Cinderella.

No, that wasn't right.

His mom had taken off early in his childhood, leaving him with a father who'd had little time to read him fairy tales. But Whit had picked up enough from movies and TV shows based on them to realize he'd gotten it wrong. If she was Cinderella, then she would be the bodyguard and not Gabriella.

"Who are you?" he asked.

Beneath the hair falling across her brow, lines of confusion furrowed. Then she blinked brown eyes wide with innocence. Real or feigned?

"You know who I am," she haughtily replied.

"No one can really know who you are," he said, "but you."

She shivered, as if his words had touched a chord deep inside her. As if he'd touched her. And he realized that he held her yet and that his fingers almost absently stroked over the silky skin of her bare shoulders. Her gown was strapless and a rich gold hue only a couple shades darker than her honey-toned skin. She was so damn beautiful.

But beauty had never affected Whit before. He wasn't like his partner—his former partner. Aaron Timmer fell quickly and easily for every pretty face. Not Whit, though. He was a professional.

So he forced himself to let go of her shoulders and step back. And that was when he heard it. Her little shuddery gasp for breath as if she'd been holding hers, too—as if she'd been waiting for him to do something. Else. Like move closer and lower his head to hers...

But besides her gasp, he heard another noise—a low thud like someone bumping into something in the dark. Despite the brightly painted walls, the sitting room was dimly lit, but small enough that Whit would have noticed someone lurking in the shadows. However, a door off the room stood ajar, darkness from her bedroom spilling out with another soft thud.

Someone was already waiting to take Princess Gabriella to bed. But she gasped again—this time with fear—and he realized she'd heard the noise, too. And she wasn't expecting anyone to be inside her bedroom.

"Stay here," he whispered and reached beneath his tuxedo jacket to pull his gun from his holster. Armed, he headed toward her bedroom.

"Be careful," she whispered back, her sweet voice trembling with concern. For him?

Her words touched something inside Whit—something that he'd closed off years ago—the part of him that had yearned to have someone—anyone—give a damn about him. Of course she didn't really care, but those words…

Distracted him enough that when he stepped inside the bedroom, the intruder got the drop on him. Before his eyes could even adjust to the darkness, something struck his head—knocking him down and knocking him out—leaving the princess at the mercy of the intruder…

BLOOD SEEPED INTO his blond hair, staining the short silky strands. Gabriella pressed her fingers to the wound, gauging the depth of it.

Would it need stitches? Had he been hit hard enough for the injury to be fatal?

She moved her fingers to his throat. He had already loosened the collar of his silk shirt and undone his bow tie, which dangled along the pleats of the shirt. So she had easy access to the warm skin of his neck. At first his pulse was faint, but then it suddenly quickened.

She glanced at his face and found his dark eyes open and staring up into hers. How could he be so blond but have such dark, fathomless eyes? The man was a paradox—a mystery that had fascinated her since the day he'd walked into the palace to guard her father.

She had been able to think of little else but him. No matter where she'd been—fashion show or gallery opening or movie premiere—her mind had been on him—which had probably made her even more distracted and nervous every time the press had interviewed her.

She had been looking forward to tonight— to seeing him in a tuxedo. To blend in, all the security team had worn black tie. But she had seen only Whit, looking like every young woman's fantasy of Prince Charming. Then her father had made his horrible pronouncement and shattered all Gabriella's illusions of a fairy-tale happily-ever-after...

"You're alive?" she asked.

While he'd opened his eyes, he had yet to move—to even draw a breath. Of course he wasn't dead, but he must have been stunned. In shock? Concussed?

Finally he nodded, then winced and repeated her ridiculous question, "You're alive?"

Her lips twitched into a smile. "I'm fine."

"The intruder didn't take you," he said, as if surprised that she wasn't gone.

"No." She shuddered at the thought of being abducted, as she had nearly been so many times before…until the former U.S. Marshal had become her bodyguard a few years ago. As well as protecting her, the ex-Marshal had taught her how to defend herself. Fortunately Gabriella hadn't been put in that position tonight. But she wished she could have defended Whit and saved him from the blow he'd taken to the head.

"Who hit me?" he asked, "Charlotte?"

She chuckled at the thought of her bodyguard knocking him out in the dark. Charlotte would not have been so cowardly, as cowardly as Gabby had been when she'd allowed her father's pronouncement at the ball to stand instead of immediately speaking up. And when she had finally gathered her courage and her anger, this man had stopped her from talking

to the king. She should have been angry with
him. But she only felt relief when he had finally opened his eyes. The three minutes he'd
been unconscious had seemed like a lifetime
to Gabby.

"Charlotte?" he repeated but his tone was
different now, as if he suspected that *she* might
actually be her bodyguard.

That was nearly as ridiculous as Charlotte
striking him. "It all happened so fast that I
have no idea who it could be. After hitting
you, he ran out the door. All I saw was that he
was dressed in black pants and a black sweat-
shirt with the hood pulled tight around his
face."

"It was a man?"

She nodded. "Tall and thin with no curves.
But I suppose it could have been a woman." At
all those fashion shows and movie premieres,
she had met many tall, thin women. "But not
Charlotte."

"No," he agreed, but tentatively, as if he debated taking her word for it.

"You don't trust me?" she asked, wondering if she should be offended or amused. Certainly it wasn't good to be thought a liar but
that wasn't the issue for her.

Most people didn't consider her clever
enough to be able to pull off any deception.

The public believed she was an empty-headed heiress. They weren't being cruel or unfair. Because she was naturally shy and introverted, nerves got the better of her during interviews, and she usually babbled incoherently—earning the nickname of Princess Gabby.

"I'm not even sure who you are," he admitted, his dark eyes narrowing with suspicion as he studied her face.

He really believed she might be Charlotte Green. Again she was flattered instead of offended. Most people might mistake the former U.S. Marshal for her—from a distance. Along with already having the same build and coloring, Charlotte had had plastic surgery so their faces looked alike, too. Except Charlotte had a beauty and wisdom that came with being six years older and so much more worldly than Gabriella. Her bodyguard was tough and independent while Gabby was anything but that.

Charlotte would not have been passed off tonight from one fiancé to another—publicly humiliated during the ball. What was worse was that the man who had traded Gabriella to the highest bidder like a brood mare at auction was her own father.

She expelled a ragged breath of frustration. "I wish I was Charlotte," she admitted. "Then I wouldn't be engaged to marry a stranger. I wouldn't have had people trying to kidnap me since I was a baby just so they could get to my father. No one would even care who I am."

"I would care," he said, with a charm of which she had not thought him capable.

She had thought him tough and cynical and dangerous and ridiculously handsome and sexy. She'd thought entirely too much of Whitaker Howell since he had stepped inside the palace ten weeks ago. She had also talked about him, asking the men he'd served with in Afghanistan to tell her about him. And the more she'd learned, the more fascinated and attracted she had become.

Now he was lying on her bedroom floor with her straddling his hard, muscular body while she leaned over him. Her fingers were still in his hair. No longer probing the wound, she was just stroking the silky blond strands.

He must have become aware of their positions, too, because his hands clasped her waist—probably to lift her off. But before he could, she leaned closer. She had to know— and since he would probably never be this vulnerable again, she had only this chance—so she pressed her mouth to his to see how he would taste.

Like strong coffee and dark chocolate—like everything too rich and not good for her. Instead of pushing her away, his hands clutched her waist and pulled her closer. And he kissed her back.

No. He took over the kiss and devoured her—with his lips and his teeth and his tongue. He left her gasping for breath and begging for more. And instead of ignoring her, as he had earlier, he gave her more. He kissed her deeply, making love to her mouth—making her want him to make love to her body. She leaned closer, pushing her breasts against his chest.

He reached for the zipper at the back of her dress, his fingers fumbling with the tab before freezing on it. "We can't do this," he said, as if trying to convince himself. "I—I need to report the intruder—need to lock down the palace and grounds…"

She would have been offended that he thought of work instead of her…if she couldn't feel exactly how much he wanted her.

"We have guests staying overnight," she reminded him. "You can't disrupt the whole palace looking for what was probably a member of the paparazzi who passed himself off as either a guest or part of the catering staff. He was probably snooping in my rooms or waiting with a camera to get some compromising photos." And if he hadn't given himself away, he might have gotten some good shots—of her and Whit.

"I still need to report the breach of security," he insisted. "And I need to make sure you have protection. Where the hell is Charlotte?"

"I gave her the night off," she said.

"And she took it?" he asked, his brow furrowing with skepticism of her claim.

"She thought I'd be safe." Because Gabriella had sworn she wouldn't leave her rooms.

His dark eyes flashed with anger. "She thought wrong."

"I will be safe," she said softly, her voice quavering with nerves that had her body trembling, as well. "If you stay with me…" She drew in a deep breath and gathered all of her courage to add, "…all night…"

SHE AWOKE ALONE in the morning—her bed empty but for the note she found crumpled under her pillow. She had obviously slept on it.

Her fingers trembled as she unfolded the paper and silently read the ominous warning: "You will die before you will ever marry the prince…"

Whitaker Howell had not left her that note. So the intruder must have. He or she hadn't been just an opportunistic guest looking for a souvenir or a member of the paparazzi looking for a story. The intruder had broken into her rooms with the intent of leaving the threat. Or of carrying it out…with Gabriella's death.

Chapter Two

Present day...

For six months Princess Gabriella St. Pierre had been missing—vanished from a hotel suite in Paris. A hotel suite that had become a gruesome crime scene where someone had died. For six months Whit Howell had been convinced *she* had been that someone. He had believed she was dead.

Just recently he'd learned that Gabby was alive and in hiding. Her life had been threatened. And instead of coming to him for protection, she had left the country. She hadn't trusted him or anyone else. But then maybe that had been the smart thing to do. Her doppelgänger bodyguard had been kidnapped in her place and held hostage for the past six months.

If Gabriella hadn't gone into hiding…

He shuddered at the thought of what might

have happened to her. But then he shuddered at the thought of what still could have happened to her since no one had heard from her for six months.

Could someone have fulfilled the prophesy of that note? The man, who had accidentally abducted the bodyguard in Gabby's place, claimed that he hadn't written it. Given all the other crimes to which he'd confessed, it made no sense that he would deny writing a note. But if not him, then who? And had that person followed through on his threat?

Whit had to find Gabby. Now. He had to make sure she was safe. He knew where she'd gone after leaving the palace. Her destination was on the piece of paper he clutched so tightly in his hand that it had grown damp and fragile.

"Sir, are you all right?" a stewardess asked as she paused in the aisle and leaned over his seat.

He nodded, dismissing her concern.

She leaned closer and adjusted the air vent over him. "You look awfully warm, sir. We'll be landing soon, but it may take a while to get to the gate."

"I'll be fine," he assured her. Because he would be closer to Gabriella—or at least closer to where she had been last. But after the woman moved down the aisle, he reached up to brush away the sweat beading on his forehead. And he grimaced over moving his injured shoulder.

He had been shot—a through-and-through, so the bullet had damaged no arteries or muscles. But now he was beginning to worry that the wound could be getting infected. And where he was going, there was unlikely to be any medical assistance.

He didn't care about his own discomfort though. He cared only about finding Gabriella and making damn sure she was alive and safe. And if he found her, he had to be strong and healthy enough to keep her safe.

Because it was probable that whoever had threatened her was still out there. Like everyone else, her stalker had probably thought her dead these past six months. But once they learned she was alive, they would be more determined than ever to carry out their threat.

"SHE'S ALIVE."

Gabriella St. Pierre expelled a breath of relief at the news Lydia Green shared the moment the older woman had burst through the door. For six months Gabby had been holding her breath, waiting for a message from her bodyguard. Actually she'd been waiting for the woman to come for her.

Especially in the beginning. She hadn't realized how pampered her life had been until she'd stayed here. The floor beneath her feet was dirt, the roof over her head thatch. A bird that had made it through her screenless window fluttered in a corner of the one room that had been her home for the past six months.

Once she had stopped waiting for Charlotte to come for her, she had gotten used to the primitive conditions. She had actually been happy here and relaxed in a way that she had never been at the palace. And it wasn't just because she had been out of the public eye but because she had been out from under her father's watchful eye, as well.

And beyond his control.

She had also been something she had never been before: useful. For the past six months she had been teaching children at the orphanage/school Lydia Green had built in a third-world country so remote and poor that no other charity or government had yet acknowledged it. But she had learned far more than she'd taught. She realized now that there was much more to being charitable than writing checks.

Lydia Green had given her life and her youth to helping those less fortunate. She'd grown up as a missionary, like her parents, traveling from third-world country to third-world country. After her parents had died, she could have chosen another life. She could have married and had a family. But Lydia had put aside whatever wants and needs she might have had and focused instead on others. She had become a missionary, too, and the only family she had left was a niece.

Charlotte. The women looked eerily similar. Lydia had the same caramel-brown eyes, but her hair was white rather than brown even though she was still in her fifties.

"Charlotte called?" The first day Gabriella had arrived, somewhere between the airport and the orphanage, she had lost the untraceable cell phone her bodyguard had given her. But it probably wouldn't have come in as far into the jungle as the orphanage was.

Lydia expelled her own breath of relief over finally hearing from her niece and nodded. "The connection was very bad, so I couldn't understand much of what Charlotte was saying…"

The orphanage landline wasn't much better than the cell phone. There was rarely a dial tone—the lines either damaged by falling trees, the oppressive humidity or rebel fighting.

"Did she tell you where she's been and why she hasn't contacted us?" Not knowing had driven Gabriella nearly crazy so that she had begun to suspect the worst—that Charlotte was dead. Or almost as bad, that Charlotte had betrayed her.

Lydia closed her eyes, as if trying to remember or perhaps to forget, and her brow furrowed. "I—I think she said she'd been kidnapped…"

"Kidnapped?" Gabby gasped the word as fear clutched at her. That would explain why they hadn't heard from the former U.S. Marshal. "Where? When?"

"It happened in Paris."

Gabriella's breath caught with a gasp. "Paris?"

She was the one who was supposed to have gone to Paris; that was what anyone who'd seen them would have believed. Whoever had abducted Charlotte had really meant to kidnap Gabby. She shuddered in reaction and in remembrance of all the kidnapping attempts she had escaped during her twenty-four years of life. If not for the bodyguards her father had hired to protect her, she probably would not have survived her childhood.

"Is she all right?"

"Yes, yes," Lydia replied anxiously, "and she said that the kidnapper has been caught."

"So I can leave…" Gabby should have been

relieved; months ago she would have been ecstatic. But since then she had learned so much about herself. So much she had yet to deal with...

"She said for you to wait."

"She's coming here?" Nerves fluttered in Gabby's stomach. She was relieved Charlotte was all right, but she wasn't ready to see her.

Or anyone else...

"She's sending someone to get you," Lydia replied, with obvious disappointment that she would not see her niece.

Gabriella was to be picked up and delivered like a package—not a person. Until she'd met Lydia and the children at the orphanage, no one had ever treated Gabriella like a person. Pride stung, she shook her head and said, "That won't be necessary."

"You're going to stay?" Lydia asked hopefully.

"I would love to," she answered honestly. Here she was needed not for *what* she was but *who* she was. She loved teaching the children. "But I can't..."

She had no idea who was coming for her, but she wasn't going to wait around to find out. Given her luck, it would probably be Whit, and he was the very last person she wanted to see. Now. And maybe ever again...

Lydia nodded, but that disappointment was back on her face, tugging her lips into a slight frown. "I understand that you have a life you need to get back to…"

Her existence in St. Pierre had never been her life; it had never been *her* choice. But that was only part of the reason she didn't plan on going back.

"But I would love to have you here," Lydia said, her voice trembling slightly, "with me…"

They had only begun to get to know each other. If they had met sooner, Gabriella's life would have been so different—so much better.

Tears burning her eyes, Gabriella moved across the small room to embrace the older woman. "Thank you…"

Lydia Green was the first person in her life who had ever been completely honest with her.

"Thank you," she said, clutching Gabriella close. "You are amazing with the kids. They all love you so much." She eased back and reached between them to touch Gabby's protruding belly. "You're going to make a wonderful mother."

The baby fluttered inside Gabriella, as if in agreement or maybe argument with the older woman's words. Was she going to make a wonderful mother? She hadn't had an example of one to emulate. Her throat choked now with tears, she could barely murmur another, "Thank you…"

She didn't want to leave, but she couldn't stay. "Can I get a ride to the bus stop in town?"

She needed a Jeep to take her to a bus and the bus to take her to a plane. It wasn't a fast trip to get anywhere in this country while the person coming for her would probably be using the royal jet and private ground transportation. She needed to move quickly.

"You really should wait for whoever Charlotte is sending for you," Lydia gently insisted. "This is a dangerous country."

Sadness clutched at her and she nodded. That was why they had so many orphans living in the dorms. The compound consisted of classroom huts and living quarters. If disease hadn't taken their parents, violence had.

"I've been safe here," she reminded Lydia.

"At the school," the woman agreed, "because the people here respect and appreciate that we're helping the children. But once you leave here…"

"I'll be fine," she assured her although she wasn't entirely certain she believed that herself.

"You have a bodyguard for a reason. Because of who you are, you're always in danger." Lydia was too busy and the country too remote for her to be up on current affairs, so Charlotte must have told her all about Gabby's life.

Gabriella glanced down at her swollen belly. Her bare feet peeped out beneath it, her toes stained with dirt from the floor. "No one will recognize me."

Not if they saw her now. She bore only a faint resemblance to the pampered princess who'd walked runways and red carpets.

But she wasn't only physically different.

She didn't need anyone to protect her anymore—especially since she really couldn't trust anyone but herself. *She* had to protect her life and the life she was carrying inside her.

A WALL OF HEAT hit Whit when he stepped from the airport. Calling the cement block building with the metal roof an airport seemed a gross exaggeration, though. He stood on the dirt road outside, choking on the dust and the exhaust fumes from the passing vehicles. Cars. Jeeps. Motorbikes. A bus pulled up near the building, and people disembarked.

A pregnant woman caught his attention. She wore a floppy straw hat and big sunglasses, looking more Hollywood than third world. But her jeans were dirt-stained as was the worn blouse she wore with the buttons stretched taut over her swollen belly.

It couldn't be Gabby.

Hell, she was *pregnant;* it couldn't be Gabby...

His cell vibrated in his pocket, drawing his attention from the woman. He grabbed it up with a gruff, "Howell here."

"Are you there?" Charlotte Green asked, her voice cracking with anxiety. "Have you found her yet?"

"The plane just landed," he replied.

He had only glanced at his phone when he'd turned it back on, but he suspected all the calls he'd missed and the voice mails he had yet to retrieve had been from the princess's very worried bodyguard.

"But Whit—"

"Give me a few minutes," he told her. "You're not even sure she's still here."

Wherever the hell *here* was; from his years as a U.S. Marine, he was well traveled but Whit had never even heard of this country before. Calling it a country was like calling that primitive building an airport—a gross exaggeration.

"I finally reached my aunt Lydia this morning," Charlotte said. "She confirmed that Gabby is still at the orphanage."

He exhaled a breath of relief. She was alive. And not lost. "That's good."

Nobody had kidnapped the princess as they had her bodyguard. Gabby was right where Charlotte had sent her six months ago. Why hadn't she answered the woman's previous calls then?

"She's all right?"

"No." Static crackled in the line, distorting whatever else Charlotte might have said.

He stopped walking, so that he didn't lose the call entirely. Reception was probably best closest to the airport, so he took a few steps back into the throng of people.

"What's wrong?" Whit asked, the anxiety all his now. "Has she been hurt?"

"Yeah…"

And he realized it wasn't static in the line but Charlotte Green's voice breaking with sobs. He had never heard the tough former U.S. Marshal cry before—not even when armed gunmen had been trying to kill them all. His heart slammed into his ribs as panic rushed through him. "Oh, my God…"

It had to be bad.

Not Gabriella…

She was the sweetest, most innocent person he'd ever met. Or at least she had been…

"Charlotte!" He needed her to pull it together and tell him what the hell had happened to the princess. In a country as primitive as this, it could have been anything. Disease. A rebel forces attack. "What's wrong?"

"It's my fault," she murmured, sobs choking her voice. "It's all my fault. I should have told her. I should have prepared her..."

"What?" he fired the question at her. "What should you have told her? What should you have prepared her for?"

The phone clanged and then a male voice spoke in his ear, "Whit, are you there?"

"Aaron?" He wasn't surprised that his fellow bodyguard was with Charlotte. Since Aaron Timmer had found her after her six-month disappearance, the man had pretty much refused to leave her side. "What's going on?"

"Don't worry about that," his fellow royal bodyguard advised. "It's just personal stuff between Charlotte and Princess Gabriella."

When the princess and her bodyguard had disappeared, Whit and Aaron had launched an extensive search to find them. Aaron had reached out for leads to their whereabouts. Whit had done the same, but he'd also dug deeply into their lives and discovered all their secrets, hoping that those revelations might lead him to them. So now he knew things about Princess Gabriella that she had yet to learn herself.

Or had she finally uncovered the truth? She must have and that was why Charlotte was so upset; she was probably full of guilt and regret. He recognized those emotions because he knew them too well himself.

"Damn it!" If that was the case, Gabby had to feel so betrayed. He added a few more curses.

"Whit," Aaron interrupted his tirade. "Just find Gabriella and bring her home to St. Pierre Island. We'll meet you there. The royal jet is about to land at the palace."

"The king is still with you?" The monarch was really their responsibility, one that both men had shirked in favor of protecting the women instead. King Rafael St. Pierre hadn't seemed to mind.

"He's secure. Everything's fine here," Aaron assured Whit. "What about there?"

"I just got off the plane." The third one. It had taken three planes—with not a single one of them as luxurious as the royal jet—over the course of three days to bring him to this remote corner of the world. And it would take a bus and a Jeep to get him to the orphanage deep in the jungle where the princess had been hiding for the past six months. "I haven't had a chance to locate Gabby and assess the situation."

Shots rang out. And he dropped low to the ground while he assessed this new situation. Who the hell was firing? And at whom? Him?

Nobody knew he'd been heading here but Charlotte and Aaron. Not that long ago he would have been suspicious; he would have considered that they might have set him up for an ambush. But the three of them had been through too much together recently. And if they'd wanted him dead, they wouldn't have had to go to this much trouble to end his life. They could have just let him bleed out from the bullet wound to his shoulder.

But the shots weren't being fired at him. They weren't that close, nowhere near the dirt street where Whit stood yet. But the shots were loud because they echoed off metal. Someone was firing inside the airport. His hand shook as he lifted the cell to his ear again.

Aaron was shouting his name. "What the hell's going on? Are those shots?"

"I'm going to check it out," he said as he headed toward the building—shoving through the wave of people running from it.

"You need to get Gabriella," Aaron shouted but still Whit could barely hear him over the shrieks and screams of the fleeing people.

Whit flashed back to that woman getting off the bus and heading inside the airport. "Gabby! Is Gabby pregnant?"

"Yes—according to Charlotte's aunt."

It was hardly something the woman would have lied about. But how? But when? And whom?

"She's probably six months along," Aaron added.

Realization dawned on Whit, overwhelming him with too many emotions to sort through let alone deal with.

Oh, God...

"That's Gabby..." Inside the airport where shots were being fired.

He shoved the phone in his pocket and reached for his gun before he remembered that he didn't have one on him. He hadn't been able to get one on the first plane he'd boarded in Michigan and hadn't had time to find one here.

Would he be able to save her? Or was he already too late?

Chapter Three

As disguises went, the hat and the glasses were weak. But it had fooled Whitaker Howell. He had barely glanced at her when she'd disembarked from the crowded bus. Of course he had seemed distracted, as he'd been reaching for his phone while moving quickly through the crowd milling from and to the airport.

She'd had to fight the urge to gawk at him. He had looked so infuriatingly handsome and sexy in a black T-shirt and jeans. But the sense of betrayal and resentment and anger overwhelmed her attraction for him. She didn't want to see Whit Howell much less be attracted to him any longer.

When she'd glimpsed him through the window, she'd thought about staying put in her seat. But since he was probably the one who'd been sent to retrieve her, he would have boarded the bus for the return trip and she would have been trapped.

When Charlotte had become her bodyguard three years ago, that was one of the first self-defense lessons she had taught Gabriella. Avoid confined places with limited exits. And given her girth, the exits on the bus had definitely been limited for her since it wasn't likely she'd been able to squeeze her belly out one of those tiny windows. So she had gotten off the bus and hurried toward the airport.

That was another of Charlotte's lessons. Stay in crowded, public places. So Gabriella had breathed a sigh of relief when she'd walked into the busy airport. She needed to buy a ticket for the first leg of the long journey ahead of her. She still had most of the cash Charlotte had given her to travel. She hadn't needed it at the orphanage. Even though she was using cash, she would still have to present identification. She fumbled inside her over-stuffed carry-on bag for the fake ID that Charlotte had provided along with the cash.

She couldn't even remember the name under which she'd traveled. Brigitte? Beverly? As she searched her bag for the wallet, she stumbled and collided with a body. A beefy hand closed around her arm—probably to steady her.

"I'm sorry," she apologized. She glanced up with a smile, but when she met the gaze of the man who'd grabbed her, her smile froze.

It wasn't Whit. He had probably already boarded the bus on its return trip to the orphanage. She didn't know this man, but from the look on his deeply tanned face, he knew her—or at least he knew of her. Most people thought her life a fairy tale; she had always considered it more a cartoon—and if that were the case, this man would have dollar signs instead of pupils in his eyes.

"Excuse me," she said and tried to pull free of the man's grasp.

But he held on to her so tightly that he pinched the muscles in her arm. "You will come with me," he told her, his voice thick with a heavy accent.

She was thousands of miles from home, but it had come to her. First Whit and now this man, who sounded as though he was either from St. Pierre Island or close to it, probably from one of the neighboring islands to which her father had promised her. Well, he'd promised her to their princes, but she would belong to the island, too. Like a possession—that was how her father treated her.

And it was how this man obviously intended to treat her. She glared at him, which, since she'd taken off her sunglasses in the dimly lit building, should have been intimidating. Charlotte hadn't had to teach her that glare—the one that made a person unapproachable. Gabriella had learned that glare at an early age—from her mother, or the woman she'd always thought was her mother.

The man, however, was not intimidated, or at least not intimidated enough to release her.

So she pulled harder, fighting his grip on her arm.

"Let me go!" she demanded, the imperious tone borrowed from her father this time. No one had ever dared refuse one of *his* commands, no matter how very much she had wanted to.

The first time he'd offered her as a fiancée she'd been too young and sheltered to understand that arranged marriages were archaic and humiliating. She'd also been friends with her first fiancé—she and Prince Linus had grown up together—spending all her holidays home from boarding school with him.

But the night of the ball her father had broken that engagement and promised her to another man, a prince who'd already been engaged to one of Gabriella's cousins. So her father had actually broken two engagements that night. He hadn't cared about the people—not that he'd ever considered her a person—he'd cared only about the politics, about using

her to link St. Pierre to another, more afflu-
ent country.

The man moved, tugging Gabriella along
with him. He pulled her through people—toward one of the wide open doors that led to the
airstrip in the back and the private planes. The
planes for which a person didn't need a ticket
or even a flight manifest in this country…

And if Gabriella got on that plane, she would
probably never get off again. Or at least she
would never be free again. Panic overwhelmed
her, pressing on her lungs so that she couldn't
draw a deep breath.

Don't panic.

Charlotte was undoubtedly still thousands
of miles away, but it was her voice in Gabriella's ear, speaking with authority and confi-
dence. And hopefully, in this case, the truth
for once.

Gabriella exhaled a shaky breath and then
dragged in a deep one, filling and expanding
her lungs with air. It was stale and heavy with
the humidity and the odor of sweaty bodies
and jet fuel and cigarette smoke. There was
no airport security to help her. She had to take
care of herself.

Assess the situation.

Despite the lies, Charlotte had helped her.
Perhaps she had even considered her lies help-

ing Gabriella, protecting her. But Charlotte had known there would be times like this when she wouldn't be there, so she had taught Gabby how to protect herself.

The man wasn't much taller than she was. But he was heavier—much heavier even with the extra pounds she was carrying in her belly. Most of his extra weight was muscle. He had no neck but had a broad back and shoulders. And at the small of his back, there was a big bulge. He had definitely come in on a private plane and from some airport with about the same level of security as this one. None.

Choose the most effective mode of protection.

Charlotte had been trained to fight and shoot and had years of experience doing both. She had taught Gabby some simple but *effective* moves. But Gabriella's experience using those methods had been in simulated fights with Charlotte, whom she hadn't wanted to hurt. Then.

A sob caught in her lungs. She didn't want to hurt her now, either. Or avoid her like she'd initially thought. She wanted to see Charlotte and talk to her, give her a chance to explain her actions and her reason for keeping so many secrets. But Gabriella couldn't do that if she didn't get the chance—if she wound up held hostage or worse.

And by effective, I mean violent...

Charlotte Green had lived a violent life, and she possessed the scars to prove it. Both physical and emotional.

Gabby only had the emotional scars until now.

She wouldn't be able to use her simulated fight moves to fend off this muscular man— probably not even if she wasn't six months pregnant. But because she was six months pregnant, she couldn't risk the baby getting hurt.

So instead she reached for the gun and pulled it from beneath the man's sweat-damp-ened shirt. The weapon was heavier than she remembered. She hadn't held one in the past six months. But before that she'd held one several times. With both hands, using one to hold and balance the gun while she focused on flicking off the safety and pulling the trig-ger with the other.

But the man held one of her hands. When he felt her grab the gun, he jerked her around and reached for the gun. So she fumbled with it quickly, sliding the safety and squeezing the trigger.

Because she hadn't wanted to hit anyone

else in the crowded airport, she'd aimed the barrel up and fired the bullet into the metal ceiling. Birds, living in the rafters, flew into a frenzy. And so did the people as the bullet ricocheted back into the cement. She breathed a sigh of relief that it struck no one. But the cement chipped, kicking up pieces of it with dust.

The man jumped, as if he'd felt the whiz of the bullet near his foot. And he lurched back. When he did, he released her arm. Now she had two hands, which she used to steady the gun and aim the barrel—this time at the man's chest.

People screamed and ran toward the exits. They thought she was dangerous. The man didn't seem to share their sentiment because he stepped forward again, advancing on her.

"I will shoot!" she warned him.

He chuckled. Then, his voice full of condescension, said, "You are a princess. What do you know of shooting guns?"

"More than enough to kill you…" Like the simulated fights, she hadn't shot a weapon with the intent of hurting anyone…except for all the targets she had killed. She was good at head shots. Even better at the heart-kill shot.

Of course those targets hadn't been moving. And the man was—advancing on her with no regard for the weapon. He was mad, too, his eyes dark with rage. If he got his hands on her again, he wasn't just going to kidnap her. He was going to hurt her. And hurting her would hurt her unborn child.

So when he lunged toward her, she fired again.

ANOTHER SHOT RANG out. But it didn't echo off metal as the earlier shot had. It was muffled—as if it had struck something. Or someone…

Gabriella…

Whit held back the shout that burned his lungs. Yelling her name might only put her in danger—if she wasn't already—or increase the danger if she was. Maybe that hadn't been Gabby he'd glimpsed getting off the bus. Maybe she was still back at the orphanage. If she'd known someone was coming for her, wouldn't she have stayed and waited?

Or maybe she hadn't wanted to be found. If the shooting involved her, she had been found, but the wrong person had done the finding. The person who'd written that threatening note?

Whit shoved through the screaming people who were nearly stampeding in their haste to escape the building. There was no sign of the pregnant woman he'd glimpsed getting off the bus. She wasn't with the others running away.

And then he saw her and realized that she was the one they were all running from—she was the one with the gun. She gripped it in both hands.

As Whit neared her, he noticed the blood spattered on her face, and his heart slammed into his ribs with fear for her safety.

"Gabby," he spoke softly, so as to not startle her, but she still jumped and swung toward him with her body and with the barrel of her gun.

He barely glanced at it, focusing instead on her face—on her incredibly beautiful face but for those droplets of blood.

Anxiously he asked, "Are you hurt?"

A groan—low and pain-filled—cut through the clamor of running people. Gabriella's lips had parted, but she was not the one who uttered the sound. Whit lowered his gaze to the man who had dropped to his knees in front of Gabby. The burly man clutched his shoulder and blood oozed between his fingers.

Whit flinched, his own shoulder wound stinging in reaction. "What the hell's going on?"

Gabby took one hand from the gun to tug

down the brim of her hat—as if her weak disguise could fool him twice.

The man took advantage of her distraction and looser grip and reached for the gun. But he could only grab at it with one hand, as his other arm hung limply from his bleeding shoulder. He had the element of surprise though and snapped it free of her grasp.

She lunged back for it, her swollen belly on the same level as the barrel of the gun. But Whit moved faster than she did and stepped between them. Before the man could move his finger to the trigger of the gun, Whit slammed his fist into the wounded man's jaw. The guy's eyes rolled back into his head as his consciousness fled, and he fell back onto the cement floor of the airport, blood pooling beneath his gunshot wound.

Whit's shoulder ached from delivering the knock-out punch, and he growled a curse. But his pain was nothing in comparison to the fear overwhelming him. He'd only just learned where Gabby was and he'd nearly lost her again.

Maybe forever this time—if the man had managed to pull the trigger before Whit had knocked him out.

"What the hell were you thinking?" he shouted the question at Princess Gabriella.

His fear wasn't for himself but for her, and he hadn't felt an emotion that intense since the night before she disappeared. The night she'd begged him to stay with her. At first he'd thought she'd only wanted protection but then he'd realized that she'd wanted more.

She'd wanted him. But then the next morning she'd left him without a backward glance. So he'd probably just been her way of rebelling against her father's attempts to control her life. That was what that night had been about, but what about today?

"I—I was defending myself," she stammered in a strangely hoarse tone, as if she'd lost her voice or was trying to disguise it. She ducked down and reached for the gun that had dropped to the floor with the man.

But Whit beat her to the weapon, clutching it tightly in his fist. "No more shooting for you, Princess."

"I'm not a princess—"

"Save it," he said. "I damn well know who you are." He had no idea why she was denying her identity to him, though. But that wasn't his most pressing concern at the moment.

He leaned over to check the man for a pulse. He was alive, just unconscious. And that might not last long. "Who is this? And why did you shoot him?"

"He tried to kidnap me," she said, apparently willing to admit that much even though she wouldn't admit to who she was. "So I grabbed his gun."

Whit uttered a low whistle of appreciation. Even without a weapon, the guy would have been intimidating, yet she'd managed to disarm him, too. Maybe she wasn't Princess Gabriella. "How do you know he was going to kidnap you?"

"He tried to drag me out there," she gestured toward the big open doors in one of the metal walls, "to a plane."

As Whit glanced up to follow the direction she pointed, he noticed men—about four of them—rushing in from the airfield. They must have heard the shots, too. And they were armed.

"We have to get the hell out of here," he said.

Or the man's friends were liable to finish what he'd started—abducting Gabriella. And Whit with his shoulder wound and his borrowed gun were hardly going to be enough protection to save her.

She must have seen the men, too, because she was already turning and moving toward the street. Whit kept between her and the men.

But they saw the guy on the ground, and they saw the gun in Whit's hand.

And they began to fire.

"WHAT'S WRONG?" Charlotte asked anxiously. "What did Whit say?"

It wasn't so much what he'd said as what Aaron had overheard when he'd been on the phone with his friend. But Charlotte was already worried about Princess Gabriella; he didn't want to upset her any more.

She settled onto the airplane seat across from him. After her trip to the restroom, her eyes were dry and clear. She'd composed herself. But how much would it take for her to break again?

She'd already been through so much—kidnapped and held hostage for six months. And she was pregnant, too, with his baby.

Aaron's heart filled with pride and love. But fear still gripped him. He wasn't like Whit; he couldn't hide his emotions. Whit usually hid them so well that Aaron had often doubted the man was even capable of feeling. But he'd heard it in his voice—his fear for Princess Gabriella's safety—once he'd realized she was also where the shooting was.

"I know something's wrong," Charlotte persisted, but she pitched her voice low and glanced toward the back of the jet where the king had retired to his private room. "Tell me."

Aaron uttered a ragged sigh of resignation and admitted, "I heard shots…"

Charlotte's eyes widened. "Someone was shooting at Whit? He wouldn't have had time to get a gun yet. He won't be able to defend himself."

On more than one occasion, Aaron had seen Whit defend himself without a gun. But he hadn't been injured then. "Whit wasn't the one getting shot at."

She gasped. "Gabby? Was it Gabby?"

"I don't know," he said. But from the way Whit had reacted to the news that the princess was pregnant, too, he was pretty sure that it was her. "It's a dangerous country. It could have been rebel gunfire. It could have been anything…"

"Call him back!" She reached across the space between them and grabbed for the cell phone he'd shoved in his shirt pocket.

But Aaron caught her hand in his and entwined their fingers. "He won't answer," he told her. "He needs to focus on what's happening. And there's nothing we can do from here anyway."

That was why he hadn't wanted to tell her. She would want to help, and that wasn't possible from so many miles away. That feeling of helplessness overwhelmed Aaron, reminding him of the way he'd felt when Charlotte had been missing. He'd been convinced that she was out there, somewhere, but he hadn't been able to find her.

Now Whit needed help—Whit, who'd so often stepped in to save him—and Aaron was too far away to come to his aid.

Panic had tears welling in her eyes. "We can have the pilot change course—"

"We're almost to St. Pierre," Aaron pointed out. "We'll be landing soon."

Panic raised her voice a couple of octaves. "Once we drop off the king, we can leave again—"

"No," he said. "There's a doctor meeting us at the palace. You need to be checked out." Even after he'd rescued her from where she'd been held hostage, she'd been through a lot.

She shook her head, tumbling those long tresses of golden brown hair around her shoulders. "I need to protect Gabby."

He knew it wasn't just because she was the princess's bodyguard. But he had to remind her, "You need to take care of our baby first."

"We shouldn't have let Whit go alone," she said. "He's hurt too badly to protect her."

"We hadn't thought she would need protecting," Aaron reminded his fiancée.

"We did," Charlotte insisted, squeezing his fingers in her distress. "Six months ago someone left her that note threatening her life. That's why I sent her into hiding." And set herself up as a decoy for the princess. Her plan had worked. Too well.

"But nobody knows where she is." Or the paparazzi would have found her, no matter where she'd been. And there would have been photographs of Princess Gabriella on every magazine and news show, as there had always been.

"If those shots were being fired at her," Charlotte said, her beautiful face tense with fear, "then someone must have figured it out."

"How?" he asked. "Nobody but you and I and Whit know where she is."

She glanced to the back of the plane. "After I talked to my aunt and confirmed that Gabby was actually still with her at the orphanage, I told the king. I thought he had a right to know."

"Was he furious?" Aaron asked. Charlotte had done much more than just violating protocol as a royal bodyguard.

"He called St. Pierre and sent out another plane with a security team as Whit's backup."

She drew in a deep breath, as if trying to soothe herself. "They should be there within a few hours."

Aaron had heard the shots. He wasn't reassured. In fact he was disheartened. He had wasted so many years being mad at Whit for something that hadn't been the man's fault. Had he repaired his friendship only to lose his friend?

If Princess Gabriella had been involved in the shooting, then Whit would have stepped in and done whatever was necessary to try to save her life—including giving up his own.

By the time the security team made it to where Whit and Gabriella were, they would probably be too late to help. With Whit injured and unarmed, it was probably already too late.

Chapter Four

Gabby pressed her palms and splayed her fingers across her belly, as if her hands alone could protect her baby from the bullets that began to fly around the airport—ricocheting off the metal roof and cement floor. She wanted to help Whit, but she had no weapon—nothing to save him. So she ran.

He returned fire as he hurried with her to the entrance. Keeping his body between her and the men, he used himself as a human shield. She would have been moved—if she hadn't known that it was bodyguard protocol to put themselves between their subject and any potential threat.

These men weren't potentially a threat; they were definitely a threat. To Whit more than to her. They probably wouldn't want to risk fatally injuring her—if they intended to kidnap her. It was hard to collect a ransom on a dead hostage. But if they'd been hired by whoever had left her that letter, then she was in as much danger as Whit was.

Maybe more.

She ran out of the building, but the street was as deserted now as the airport was. All the people had scattered and left. It was no safer out here than it had been in the deserted metal building.

But she had Whit. He'd stayed with her, his hand on her arm—urging her forward—away from the danger. But the danger followed them. Shots continued to ring out. Whit's gun clicked with the telltale sound of an empty magazine. He cursed.

Panic slammed through Gabby. The men chasing them were not about to run out of bullets—not with all the guns they had. Should she and Whit stop and lift their arms in surrender and hope they were not killed? Before she could ask Whit, he made the decision for them.

He lifted her off the ground and ran toward the street. Gabby didn't wriggle and try to fight free as she had six months ago. Instead of pounding on him, she clutched at him, so that he wouldn't drop her. He leaned and ducked down, as if dodging bullets.

Gabriella felt the air stir as the shots whizzed past. But with the way he was holding her—she wouldn't feel the bullets. They would have to pass through Whit's body before hitting hers. Again, it was bodyguard protocol, but she couldn't help being impressed, touched and horrified that he might get killed protecting her.

He ran into the street, narrowly avoiding a collision with a Jeep. The vehicle screeched to a halt, and Whit jerked open the passenger door and jumped inside. He deposited her in the passenger seat and forced his way into the driver's seat, pushing the driver out of the door.

The man scrambled to his feet and cursed at him. Then he ducked low and ran when the gunmen rushed up behind him, firing wildly at the vehicle. Whit slammed his foot on the gas, accelerating with such force that Gabriella's back pressed into the seat. She grabbed for the seat belt, but there wasn't one.

"Hang on tight," Whit advised.

She stretched out her arms and braced her hands on the dash, so that she wouldn't slam into it and hurt the baby. "Please, hurry," she pleaded. "Hurry—before they catch up to us."

"Where the hell am I going?" he asked. "Which way to the orphanage?"

Panic shot through her, shortening her breath as she thought of the danger. "No. No. We can't—we can't risk leading these men back to the orphanage." Those children had already lost so much to violence; she wouldn't let them get caught in the cross fire and lose their lives, too.

"I'll make sure we're not followed," Whit assured her. "But we have to hurry."

She hesitated. She'd been uncertain that she could trust anyone again, let alone him. But this wasn't her heart she was risking. It was so much more important than that. Whit was good at his job. Charlotte wouldn't have had the king hire him if he and Aaron hadn't been good bodyguards. So she gave him directions, leading him deeper and deeper into the jungle.

The Jeep bounced along the rutted trails, barely passing between the trees and the other foliage that threatened the paths. Gabby left one hand on the dash and reached for the roll bars over her head with the other, holding tight, so that she didn't risk an injury to her unborn child. She also kept turning around to check the back window and make certain that they had not been followed.

"No one's behind us," Whit assured her with a glance at the rearview mirror. "I've been watching."

She uttered a breath of relief that they wouldn't be leading danger back to the orphanage. At the speed that Whit was driving, they arrived in record time at the complex of huts and larger wood-and-thatch buildings that comprised the orphanage.

"This is it," she said with a surge of pride and happiness, which was the polar opposite from the way she'd felt when she'd first seen the complex six months ago. When she'd accepted that it was really where Charlotte had sent her, her heart had been heavy with dread and her pulse quick with panic. "We're here."

Whit stepped on the brake but didn't put the transmission into Park. Instead he peered through the dust-smeared windshield at the collection of crude outbuildings that made up the orphanage complex.

"This is it?" he echoed her words but his deep voice was full of skepticism.

"This is it," she confirmed. Now that she knew how hard it was to build in the jungle, she was even more impressed with what Lydia had achieved—and with what Gabriella had helped her manage during her stay. "Pull around the back of that hut. That's mine."

He followed her direction, parking the Jeep where she pointed. But before she could open her door, he reached across her. His hand splayed over her belly. He leaned close, so close that she felt his breath warm her face when he asked, "Is this mine?"

She shivered at his closeness and the intensity in his dark eyes. But she couldn't meet his gaze and lie to him. So she glanced down and noticed the blood that trickled down his arm. And she gasped in shock and horror. "You were shot!"

Perhaps it had only been his duty as a royal bodyguard, perhaps it had been his concern for the child he suspected might be his—but he'd taken a bullet that had been meant for her. And after being hit, he'd driven the Jeep over tough terrain to get them to safety.

"We need to get you inside," she said, fighting back her panic and concern. During her time at the orphanage, she'd learned to not let the children see her anxiety when they were hurt because it only upset and hurt them more. "And I'll have Lydia call for the doctor."

She opened the door and slipped out from under his hand. Then she hurried around to the driver's side and opened his door.

In addition to the blood trailing down his arm and turning the shoulder of his shirt an even darker black with wetness, he had sweat beading on his brow and upper lip. It was hot and humid in the jungle. But she'd heard the other guards talking about Whit's deployments to the Middle East—usually because she had asked them to tell her about the blond bodyguard—and they had always said how he had never perspired—not in the heat—not under pressure.

Was he hurt that bad?

She lifted his arm and slid beneath it, in order to help him from the driver's seat. But he didn't lean on her. With a short grunt of pain, he unfolded himself from beneath the wheel and stepped out of the Jeep to stand beside her. Close beside her, his tense body nearly touching hers. He leaned down, so that their gazes met and locked.

"I don't need a doctor," he said, dismissing her concern. "I need the truth."

She had given up denying her identity to him. She'd only been able to fool him once, but he obviously had no doubt about who she was now. So what did he mean? "The truth about what?"

His throat moved, rippling, as if he swallowed hard. And after clearing his throat, he asked, "Is that baby you're carrying mine?"

The baby shifted inside her, kicking at her belly, as if he, too, wanted to know the answer. She placed her palms over her stomach again, protectively. And because she felt so protective, she wasn't willing to share her baby with anyone.

Not even the baby's father.

Whit moved to lift his arms—probably to grab her and maybe shake the truth out of her—but the movement had his handsome face contorting with a grimace of pain. And a groan slipped from between his gritted teeth.

"Doctor first," she insisted. "Then we'll talk…"

Maybe by the time she had Lydia summon the doctor from the clinic in the more populated town close by, she would have figured out if she was going to tell Whit the truth.

WHIT GLANCED DOWN at the dirt floor beneath his feet and peered up at the thatched roof. The hut was primitive and small. There was only enough space for the double bed that stood in the middle of the room, enshrouded in a canopy of mosquito netting. He sat on the edge of that bed, so he had a clear view out the window and the doorway. To make sure no one had followed them from the airport.

There was no screen or glass in the window; it was just a hole to the jungle. There was no door either—just the threshold through which Gabby passed as she returned from wherever she'd gone to summon a doctor.

Her bodyguard had sent her here to keep her safe? Anger at Charlotte Green coursed through him. Any animal—two-legged or four-legged—from the jungle could have come inside and dragged her off never to be seen again. After he had learned all the secrets about Gabriella St. Pierre, he'd begun to question Charlotte's motives. Now he questioned them again.

"This is where you've been staying?" he asked, still shocked that the princess of St. Pierre would have spent one night in such primitive conditions let alone six months.

Gabby glanced around the tiny hut, and her lips curved into a wistful smile. "Yes…"

Not only had she stayed here but she seemed to have actually enjoyed it.

"I'm sorry I was gone so long," she said, "but Lydia was with a class. My class, actually." Her smile widened. "And the children were so thrilled that I came back…"

"You've been teaching here?"

"Yes, it's a school as well as an orphanage." She peered through that hole in the wall as if checking the jungle for threats. "Are you certain that no one followed us?"

"They would have been here already," he pointed out. Because they would have had to follow them directly from the airport in order to find this place. But he looked out the window, too. "You're safe."

"It's not me I'm worried about…" Her palms

slid over her belly, as if protecting or comforting the child within. "Those kids have already been through so much…"

When he had first met Princess St. Pierre, he had been impressed that someone as privileged and probably pampered as she must have been seemed to actually care about people. She had showed genuine interest in the lives of the palace staff. But here she had taken that interest to a whole other level, sacrificing her own comfort to care for others. She wasn't just a princess; she was a saint.

He had nothing to offer a princess; he had even less to offer a saint. All he could give Princess Gabriella St. Pierre was his protection. He stared at her belly. Unless he'd already given her something else…

He opened his mouth to ask again the question that had been burning in his mind since the minute he had realized the pregnant woman from the bus was Princess Gabriella. Was that baby his?

But before he could ask, she hurriedly said, "The doctor should be here soon. The clinic is just a mile away."

"I don't need a doctor."

"You've been shot," she said, moving her hands from her belly to his arm.

Blood still trickled slowly from the old

wound in his shoulder, over his biceps, down his forearm, over his wrist to drip off his fingertips onto the dirt floor.

"Yes, I was shot," he admitted with a wince of pain as he remembered the burn of the bullet ripping through his flesh. "But not today."

Her brow furrowed in confusion. "But you're bleeding…"

He shrugged and then winced again as pain radiated throughout his shoulder and his fingers tingled in reaction. "The wound must have reopened."

"When you carried me…"

Despite the men chasing them, firing shots at them, he had enjoyed carrying her. He had savored her slight weight in his arms, the heat of her body pressed against his, her hands clutching at him—holding him close. It had reminded him of that night—that night he had taken on the responsibility of guarding her.

But he hadn't really protected her…not if that child was his. He groaned.

"You are hurting," she said and commanded him, "Take off your shirt." But she didn't wait for him to obey her royal order. She lifted his T-shirt, her fingers grazing his abdomen and then his chest as she pulled the damp fabric over his head. Expelled in a gasp, her breath whispered across his skin.

Despite the oppressive heat, he nearly shivered in reaction to her touch. For six interminable, miserable months he'd thought she was dead. He had thought he would never see her again. That he would never touch her...

Was she real? She was so beautiful that he doubted it, as he had the first time he'd met her. She couldn't be real. Maybe he had been shot again, and this time he'd died and found an angel. He snorted in derision of his ridiculous thought. As if he would ever make it to heaven...

"This wound isn't very old," she observed, her teeth nibbling at her bottom lip with concern. "When were you shot?"

"Five or six days ago..." He couldn't remember exactly; everything had happened so quickly and then it had taken him so many days and flights to reach her. Maybe he should have waited for one of the royal jets to be available. But the king had needed to return to St. Pierre so he had taken his, and Whit hadn't wanted to wait for one to come in from St. Pierre. He hadn't wanted to wait another minute to see Gabriella and make sure she was safe. He had never imagined he'd find the Princess of St. Pierre like this...

Literally barefoot and pregnant.

"You should be in the hospital," she admonished him, as she rose up on tiptoe and inspected his wound.

"I saw a doctor already," he assured her. "I'm all stitched up. I'm fine." So they could talk. And maybe he would have insisted on it already if he wasn't worried about what she would tell him. Several years ago he had sworn he would never become a father. Or a husband. He'd had no intention of ever attempting a long-term relationship.

"You were shot!" she snapped at him, temper flashing in her eyes. "How did that happen?"

He shrugged and then cursed as the movement jostled his wounded shoulder, sending pain radiating down his arm until his fingers tingled.

Damn it...

He shouldn't be the one to tell her any of this. He was only supposed to retrieve her from her hiding spot and bring her back to the opulent palace on St. Pierre Island. Then her father and her bodyguard could explain everything...

The king and the others had probably landed on St. Pierre by now, so they could send the royal jet here. And Whit could bring her home where she belonged—with her family and her fiancé. He grabbed his cell phone from the front pocket of his jeans, but the screen was illuminated with a disheartening message. No service.

"That's not going to work," she informed him. "You're not stalling…"

"Stalling?" he scoffed. "I'm trying to call the palace."

Her breath caught, and her eyes widened with panic.

And he realized something. "You weren't in that airport to take a flight home."

"Home?" she repeated.

"The country of which you're the princess," he reminded her. "Where you grew up, where you live…"

"I grew up in a boarding school," she said. "And I've been living here."

At another boarding school/orphanage. Was that how she'd felt growing up? Like an orphan? Or was that feeling new because of what she might have learned about herself and all those secrets he'd uncovered?

"You know what I mean," he said. "You weren't heading back to St. Pierre." She'd been running again. And that was probably why she had worn the disguise and tried to deny her identity to him. She hadn't wanted him to bring her back to St. Pierre.

Instead of denying his claim, she changed

the subject. "Tell me why you were shot," she urged him. "I know Charlotte was kidnapped. The telephone connection was bad but Lydia understood that much."

And knowing that, she hadn't intended to go back to St. Pierre? Charlotte's concern that Gabby was upset with her might have been warranted.

"I know Charlotte's safe now," Gabriella said, as if she'd read his mind.

Or his expression, which would have been odd given that everyone—even those to whom he'd been closest—always claimed that he had a poker face, that they could never tell what he was thinking or feeling. Or if he even felt anything.

"The kidnapper was caught," she continued. "Did you get shot rescuing Charlotte from him?"

"Aaron rescued her," he said. Because his fellow royal bodyguard was madly in love with Charlotte. "I got shot when we went back to where she'd been held captive and tried to discover who was behind the kidnapping."

She drew in a quick, sharp breath. "But he was caught, right?"

He nodded, wishing again that he'd been part of the takedown. But he'd been knocked out cold from the painkillers the doctor who'd stitched up his gunshot wound had given him.

"Who was it?" she asked, her eyes wide with fear. She must have figured out that she—not Charlotte—had been the kidnapper's intended hostage.

He drew in a deep breath, hoping to distract her. He was only responsible for her safety, not a debriefing. "We need to get back to St. Pierre, and the others can explain everything."

Anger flashed in her eyes again, and she narrowed them. "If you're not going to tell me what I want to know, why should I tell you?"

Debriefing wasn't part of his job, but he hadn't made any promises to lie to her. Only to keep her safe. "The kidnapper was Prince Linus Demetrios."

She gasped at the name of her ex-fiancé. "No. Linus wouldn't have shot you. He would never hurt anyone. He's not capable..."

As sheltered as her life had been, she had no idea of what desperate men were capable. He hoped she never found out.

"He actually wasn't responsible for my gunshot wound," Whit admitted. "But he was responsible for Charlotte's kidnapping."

"He thought she was me?" she asked, her voice cracking with emotion and those dark eyes filling with guilt.

He didn't want to tell her, didn't want to make her feel worse. But he wouldn't lie to her, as everyone else had. So he just nodded.

"But why would Linus want to kidnap me?"

"He didn't want to lose you," Whit said. While he didn't appreciate the man's methods, he understood his reasoning.

"How was kidnapping me going to keep me?" she asked. "Did he intend to never let me go? To hold me captive forever?"

Whit sighed and figured he might as well explain the man's twisted plan as best he understood it. "He intended to get you pregnant, so he would have a claim to St. Pierre through an heir."

Hurt flashed across her face. "Of course he didn't really want me. He wanted my country." Her eyes widened with shock. "Did he…hurt Charlotte?"

"No. He was going to go about it artificially, but she was already pregnant—"

"Charlotte's pregnant, too?"

"Yes," he said. "With Aaron's baby."

Her pain and indignation forgotten, she smiled. "That's wonderful. And the baby is all right despite her being abducted?"

"Fine," he assured her. "She's fine. You can see for yourself soon enough."

She shook her head. "No…"

Was she refusing to return or was she denying something else entirely? "What do you mean?"

"That plan couldn't have been Linus's alone. He wasn't that clever or that conniving," she said. "But his father..."

"His father?" At the ball, he'd been warned to be especially vigilant of King Demetrios after Gabby's father made his announcement changing her engagement. The man had been enraged, but he hadn't spoken a word, just left in a blind fury.

"King Demetrios was determined to join his country to St. Pierre," she explained. "He could have masterminded the whole plot."

And if that plot had been thwarted, would he have stepped in again with the help of the man who tried grabbing Gabby in the airport? Maybe his son's arrest hadn't stopped his machinations.

"Is everything all right?" a woman's voice— as soft and sweet as Gabby's—asked.

Whit turned toward the doorway, toward the woman who, except for having white hair instead of golden brown, looked exactly like Gabby. He glanced from her to the princess and back—just in confirmation of what he already knew.

And seeing the look of understanding and

betrayal on Gabriella's face, she realized that he'd known. And anger chased away her guilt.

THE SENSE OF betrayal overwhelmed Gabriella. She'd told herself that Whit wouldn't have known—that he might not have been keeping secrets like everyone else in her life had. But when he'd looked from her to Lydia and back, he hadn't been surprised by their uncanny resemblance.

He'd known that they were related. He'd known that Charlotte Green was more than Gabby's bodyguard; she was her sister, too—an illegitimate princess.

But then so was Gabby. Just like the baby she carried was an illegitimate royal. She pressed her palms over her belly as the baby shifted inside her, kicking so hard that Gabby's stomach moved. Her sister was also pregnant, her baby probably conceived the same night that Gabby's had been.

Gabriella was happy for her, but she didn't want to be with her. Not yet. Six months hadn't been long enough for her to come to terms with how she had been betrayed—by her father. By her sister...

She hadn't thought of Charlotte as just her bodyguard; she'd considered her a friend. She'd been such a fool...

Whit had gone with Lydia back to her office, so that he could use the landline phone—so that he could call for the royal jet to take her back to St. Pierre. He'd saved her from a kidnapper only to kidnap her himself—to take her somewhere she didn't want to be.

She glanced out through that open window to where he'd parked the Jeep. The keys dangled from the ignition. During the past six months, she'd learned to drive a manual transmission.

She grabbed up her backpack from the bed and headed out to the Jeep. It would take a while for Whit to get his call through, and even longer for him and whoever he called to understand what each other was saying. By the time he finished with his call, she would be almost back to the airport.

Authorities must have been called. Someone would have reported the shooting and Whit stealing the Jeep. With the local police swarming the airport, nobody would try to kidnap her again. She would probably be safer there than here with Whit.

But her hand trembled with nerves as she lifted the handle and pulled open the door. She stepped up into the Jeep and slid beneath the wheel. But before she could swing the door shut behind herself, a strong hand jerked it from her grasp.

She didn't look to confirm her fear of being abducted. But that hand couldn't belong to Whit. He couldn't have returned to the hut yet.

Had the men actually followed them but stayed out of sight until they'd found her—alone and vulnerable?

Chapter Five

Whit had left her alone and vulnerable. Some damn bodyguard he was.

And when he had stepped inside her hut and found it empty, he'd felt every bit as sick as he had when he'd seen that trashed hotel suite in Paris. The walls had been riddled with bullets, the rug and hardwood floor saturated with blood. He'd thought her dead then.

He didn't think her dead now. He thought her pissed off. So he wasn't surprised to find her trying to take off in the Jeep.

But she was surprised to see him. Her lips parted in a gasp when he stopped the door from closing. Then he reached for her.

She slapped at his hand and then turned, kicking out with her leg. Her foot connected squarely with his kneecap, which caused his knee to buckle and nearly give beneath his weight.

"Damn it!" he cursed her. And Charlotte.

Her bodyguard had taught her some self-defense moves—in addition to teaching her how to shoot.

If the guy in the airport hadn't been trying to abduct her, Whit might have felt sorry for him taking the bullet in his shoulder. He knew too well how that felt. His throbbed with pain, but he ignored the discomfort as he tugged her from the vehicle. "Where the hell do you think you're going?"

"Whit?" She finally focused on him, her eyes widening with surprise. She stopped fighting and allowed him to guide her back inside the hut. "I thought you were calling St. Pierre."

St. Pierre. Not home.

Whit could relate. He'd never really had any place he had called home. After his mom had left, he and his dad had moved around a lot—his dad following the seasonal work of construction. Then Whit had joined the marines, going from base to base, deployment to deployment. And becoming a bodyguard had brought Whit into other people's homes without ever giving him a chance to make one of his own.

"Your aunt is making the call for me," he said. He had asked her to the moment he'd realized he shouldn't have left Gabby alone—because of her safety both physically and emotionally.

"You know who she is." Her usually sweet soft voice was sharp with resentment, and her eyes darkened with anger. "You were just like everyone else keeping secrets from me and using me."

Not only was she angry, she was in pain, too. He reached for her, trying to close his arms around her to offer comfort and assurance. "I didn't—"

But she jerked away from him, as if unable to bear his touch. But then she touched him, pressing her palms against his chest to push him back.

"How could you…" her voice cracked with emotion "…how could you be with me that night and not tell me what you knew?"

If anyone had used anyone that night, she had used him—probably to get back at her father for humiliating her at the ball. She must have figured having his daughter sleep with the hired help would shame the king.

"I didn't know, that night, that you and Charlotte were related," he said. But he should have noticed the resemblance sooner since he'd known the U.S. Marshal before her plastic surgery; the surgeon hadn't had to change much to make her Gabby's virtual twin.

She stared at him, her eyes still narrowed with skepticism. She probably thought he should have known, too.

He continued, "I didn't find out until after you'd disappeared." And remembering his anguish over that, his temperature rose and his blood pumped faster and harder in his veins. She'd let him and her father and her fiancé believe she was dead. She was hardly the saint he'd painted her to be. "How could you?"

"How could I what?" she asked, her brow furrowing with confusion.

Images of that hotel suite flashed through his mind again, bringing back all those feelings of fear and loss and…

"How could you just take off?" he asked. And leave everyone behind worried sick about her.

"I had a threat," she replied. "That person who hit you over the head that night left something under my pillow."

"A letter threatening your life," Whit said. If she hadn't distracted him from doing his job that evening, he would have been the one to find the note. Or if he'd followed his instincts and locked down the palace, he might have found the person who'd left the threat. "I know."

"Then you must know why I disappeared," she said, as if he were an idiot unable to grasp a simple concept. "I was in danger."

"Still are." His gut tightened with dread at the thought of that man pointing the gun at her and her unborn baby.

She shook her head. "The kidnapper was caught."

"Then who were those men at the airport?" he asked. "They sure as hell looked dangerous to me. Then again I didn't get a good look at them—I was too busy dodging the bullets they were firing at us."

"They probably thought we'd killed their friend," she said, making excuses for the men. "I shot him, and you knocked him out."

Whit nodded. "Yes, because he was threatening your life—just like the person who'd left the note. So you are definitely still in danger."

She shrugged, apparently unconcerned. "The man who grabbed me was an opportunist. He recognized me, saw that I was unprotected and tried to take advantage of the situation."

"Why was he here?" Why? Had he followed Whit right to her? And if he'd followed him from the place Charlotte Green had been held captive in Michigan, then he could have followed him to the orphanage.

"This country is a war zone full of rebels and mercenaries," Gabriella said.

"Then why the hell would your bodyguard send you here?" Maybe his doubts about Charlotte's motives had been right. Maybe she hadn't been trying to protect Princess Gabriella when she'd had plastic surgery to look just like her; maybe she had been trying to take her place as the legitimate heir to the country of St. Pierre and the fortune of the king.

But Charlotte had seemed to genuinely care about her assignment. About her *sister.* Then he realized the answer to his own question. "She couldn't tell you. The king had sworn her to secrecy with the threat of firing her if she told you the truth."

Gabriella gasped and then blinked furiously as tears pooled in her eyes. "My father wouldn't allow her to tell me?"

He had begun to appreciate Charlotte Green when she'd saved his life four or five days ago. But he really appreciated her now, for finding a way around the king's royal decree. "So she showed you. She had to know that once you met her aunt you would figure it out."

Charlotte had found a way around the king, but with the way she'd handled the situation,

Gabriella had been alone when she'd learned the truth. Even though Lydia was related to her, she was a stranger. There had been no one there for Gabby who could have held her, who could have comforted her.

His arms ached, not from the gunshot wound, but with the need to hold her, to have been the one who comforted her when her world had turned on its axis. And when everything that she had believed to be true had become a lie.

She expelled a shaky breath. "I figured out that my father, that *my family,*" her voice cracked as emotion overwhelmed her, "has made a fool of me my entire life."

He reached for her again, and this time she didn't fight him off. Instead she wrapped her arms around his shoulders and clung to him. And his arms, which had ached to hold her, embraced her.

He ignored the twinge of pain in his shoulder. He ignored everything but how warm and soft she was and how perfect she felt.

Then, even as close as they were, there was a movement between them. The baby shifted in her stomach, kicking him as he or she kicked Gabby. While it was only a gentle movement, Whit felt the kick more violently than he had the princess's when she'd tried to fight him off at the Jeep.

This baby inside her could possibly be his. He could be a father?

GABBY FELT HIM tense, so she pulled back—embarrassed that she had clung to him. More embarrassed that she'd wanted to keep clinging to him. She had missed him, missed his touch—his strength. That night he'd guarded her he had made her feel safer than she'd ever felt. He'd made her feel *more* than she had ever felt.

Even now, her tumultuous emotions were all mixed up about him. She had to remind herself that, like that night, he was just doing his job. She meant nothing more to him than a paycheck from her father. She'd realized that when she'd woken alone the next morning and even more so when she'd left for Paris and he hadn't tried to stop her.

She'd felt like such a fool for throwing herself at a man who really hadn't wanted her. And then she had come here…and discovered exactly how big a fool she'd been.

"I could never figure out why my mother—the queen—hated me so much," she admitted.

The woman had never shown Gabby an ounce of affection or approval. On her deathbed, she had even refused to see Gabriella—not wanting hers to be the last face she ever saw. She had never been able to tolerate even looking at Gabby. That was why she'd sent her off to boarding schools when she'd been scarcely more than a toddler.

"But she wasn't really my mother," Gabriella said. She had actually been relieved to learn that; it had explained so much. It wasn't just that she was so unlovable her own mother hadn't been able to love her. The queen hadn't been her mother. But then her biological mother hadn't loved her either since she'd so easily given up her baby.

"The queen couldn't have any children," she continued. He undoubtedly already knew this, but she needed to say it aloud—needed to bring the secrets to light since she had been left in the dark too long. "So the king had his mistress give him another baby—one he intended to claim and make the queen pretend was hers. Unlike Charlotte, whom he never claimed."

"He has now," Whit said, as if it mattered.

The king had denied the paternity of his eldest for thirty years. And for twenty-four years he'd denied Gabby a relationship with her sister and her aunt. Gabriella would never be able to forgive him that—let alone having traded her from one fiancé to another like livestock. But, as things had turned out, he had been right to break her engagement to Prince Linus. Despite her friendship with him, he hadn't been the man she'd thought he was.

Even if he hadn't masterminded the kidnapping plot, he had gone along with it. He'd put Charlotte's life and the life of Gabby's future niece or nephew at risk. But he hadn't done it out of love. He'd done it so he could make a claim on her country.

Nobody in her life had actually been the person she'd thought he or she was.

As if on cue, Lydia Green stepped through the doorway and entered the hut. Her gaze went immediately to Gabby, as if surprised to find her still there and emotionally intact.

Gabby was surprised, too. But then if Whit hadn't caught her, she might have been halfway to the airport by now.

"Did the call go through?" Whit asked.

Gabby held her breath, hoping that it hadn't. She didn't want the royal jet being sent for her—because she knew there was only one place that jet would bring her. Back to St. Pierre.

But Lydia nodded. Her gaze still on Gabby, her eyes filled with regret. She knew this wasn't what Gabriella wanted. She was the first one who actually cared what Gabby wanted.

"When are they going to send the royal jet?" Whit asked.

Her aunt still wouldn't look at him, continuing to stare at Gabby—much as she had the first time Gabriella had shown up at the orphanage. When her sister had signed off her parental rights to her youngest child, Lydia had thought she would never see the baby again. She had been elated when she'd realized who Gabriella really was.

Gabby had been devastated. Her biological mother had basically sold her. Unlike Lydia who'd followed her parents into missionary work, Bonita Green had resented never having material possessions. She'd spent her life conning people out of theirs until one of those marks had cut her life short.

Gabby would never have the chance to meet the woman—not that she ever would have wanted to. The queen and a former con artist were her only maternal examples. Gabby rubbed her belly, silently apologizing to her baby. It wasn't really a question of if she would screw up; it was more a question of how badly.

"Are they going to send it?" Whit anxiously prodded Lydia for a reply.

Her aunt continued to focus on Gabby.

"They already sent it—several hours ago actually. It should be here soon."

She obviously wondered if Gabby still wanted to go. Gabby had actually never intended to go back there. But she wasn't going to put Lydia in the awkward position that Charlotte had when she'd sent Gabby here. So she nodded her acceptance and forced a smile.

Her aunt released a soft sigh, but Gabby couldn't tell if it was of relief or disappointment.

"Before you leave for the airport, come say goodbye," Lydia said, "again."

"We will," Whit answered for them both.

Once her aunt had gone, Gabby admonished him, "You shouldn't have spoken for me."

His jaw tensed; perhaps he clenched his teeth in response to her imperious tone. But he didn't apologize or argue. He only headed for the doorway, as if she were going to blindly follow him.

"I'm not leaving," she explained. She had no intention of going where she couldn't trust anyone.

THE WOMAN INFURIATED him. From the moment he'd met her, he hadn't been able to figure her out. She was unlike anyone else he'd ever known. "If you're not leaving, why the hell did I just stop you from taking off in the Jeep?"

"I was trying to get away from you," she said dispassionately, as if her words weren't like a knife plunged in his back.

"Why?"

"Because I can't trust you," she said—again so matter-of-factly that it was obvious she had never considered trusting him at all.

But before he could defend himself, she continued, "I can't trust anyone on St. Pierre. That's why I'm not going back."

He understood her reasons. But he had a job to do—protect her. And after the close call at the airport, he wasn't convinced he could do that alone. Especially not here. He had a gun but no bullets, a shoulder throbbing with pain and a possible infection. "You can't stay here."

She let out a wistful sigh. "I know."

She'd been leaving earlier, and in a disguise, because everyone knew where she was now. He couldn't blame her for wanting to stay hidden.

"Where were you going?" he asked again.

She chuckled but without humor. "You really are just like everyone else," she mused. "You think I'm an idiot. But you shouldn't believe my image. It's a lie just like the rest of my life has been."

He'd already learned that for himself.

She lifted her chin with stubbornness and pride. "I'm not telling you where I'm going."

"Fine," he said. "I'll tell *you*. You're going with me." Back to St. Pierre? Could he bring her back there? To the family who'd lied to her? To the stranger she didn't want to marry?

His stomach churned with revulsion over the thought of her marrying anyone, of her lying in anyone else's bed, in anyone else's arms…

He forced away the repugnance and the twinges of jealousy. He had no right to either. Unless…

"We are leaving," he continued. "As soon as you tell me who the father of your baby is."

She flinched, as if he'd slapped her. Or insulted her. Because she'd often been photographed with movie stars and athletes, the media had painted her as a promiscuous princess. But he had intimately learned exactly how wrong they had been about her—as wrong as when they'd claimed she was ditzy.

She was neither.

"You've been working for my father too long," she said. From the disdain in her voice, the comment was obviously more complaint than compliment. "You're beginning to act just like him."

He winced now, definitely offended. Fortunately he had only been hired to protect the man, not to like him. King St. Pierre was tough to like. He was a difficult man. Period.

"Since I do work for your father, I need to carry out his orders," Whit replied, choosing to ignore the insult and focus on what was more important. "He wants you safely back in St. Pierre."

She snorted—a sound he would have thought her entirely too ladylike to make. Wouldn't some princess etiquette class in one of those fancy boarding schools she'd attended have polished the ability to snort right out of her?

She lifted her chin again, looking every bit the royal ruler despite her dirty jeans and blouse. "You're crazy to think I will be safe in St. Pierre."

He might have agreed with her if he hadn't just re-established his friendship with Aaron. He trusted that man with his life and hers. "You'll be safer there than you are here where you were just nearly abducted and shot at…"

She might have been right about it being a crime of opportunity. Maybe it was just a dangerous country with dangerous men. Maybe he hadn't been followed straight to her…

"That can happen in St. Pierre, too," she pointed out.

"I will make sure it doesn't happen," he said. "I will protect you." And with Aaron and Charlotte helping, he had a good possibility of actually keeping her safe.

"You will protect me from kidnappers and killers," she agreed—again with that damn calmness that infuriated him. "But will you protect me from my father?"

He couldn't say that her father wouldn't hurt her—because he already had. With his lies. With his manipulations…

Maybe she had learned some of her father's moves because she had veered the conversation away from what he wanted to know. She'd stalled him long enough. Maybe it was her form of payback for having had to wait twenty-four years before she'd learned the truth.

"Gabby," he began, about to urge her to stop the cycle of secrets now.

But the roar of a Jeep engine drew his attention to the doorway. If he'd missed a tail from the airport, he had lost his ability to do his job properly—then he couldn't protect the princess.

But there was only one man in the Jeep. Both the man and the vehicle must have been familiar to the kids because they came out of nowhere to greet him, dancing around his feet like puppies as he hopped out of the vehicle.

The kids hadn't greeted him and Gabby like that. Maybe they'd been in class. Or maybe they had been taught to never approach a strange vehicle or a strange man. This man wasn't unfamiliar to them.

Despite the black medical bag clutched in his hand, he looked too young to be a doctor.

Whit should have cancelled the house call Lydia had arranged; he didn't need a doctor. He needed the truth from the princess; he needed to know the paternity of her baby.

"Gabriella," the man said. With the familiarity of a frequent visitor, he stepped through the hut doorway without knocking and waiting for her permission to enter. "I am sorry I took so long getting away from the clinic."

She offered this man the smile she used to give Whit when they'd first met. It was a smile full of warmth and welcome and beauty. Whit wondered if she would ever smile that way at him again.

"Dominic, it's fine," she assured the doctor, her concern for Whit's injury obviously long forgotten. "I know how busy you are."

The guy answered her smile with a wide grin. Not only was he young but good-looking, too, since women seemed to like that whole tall and dark thing. Or at least that was what he'd witnessed with the women who'd gone for Aaron Timmer over the years. As easily as his partner had fallen for women, they had responded to him, too.

This guy also had charm. His grin widened as he took Gabby's hand in his with a familiarity and possessiveness that had Whit gritting his teeth. "If you had been the patient, I would have dropped everything…"

For her. Not for Whit. The doctor had clearly fallen for the princess.

Maybe Whit had been wrong to assume the child she carried was his. Maybe her baby belonged to this man.

Whit should have been relieved that he might not be the father. But his heart dropped with regret. And then possessiveness gripped him.

He did not want Princess Gabriella or the baby she carried belonging to any man but him.

Chapter Six

"The doctor gave me a clean bill of health."

Aaron Timmer grinned at the news. He was apparently as relieved as she was that their baby was all right. But Charlotte wasn't worried only about the baby she carried. She was worried about the baby sister she'd failed to protect as she'd sworn she would.

"I'm clear to travel," she said. "Clear to do my job."

Aaron shook his head. "You don't have a job anymore," he reminded her. "The king doesn't want you working for him."

King St. Pierre claimed that he wanted Charlotte as a daughter now, not as an employee. But she worried that he'd dismissed her because he no longer trusted her to safeguard the princess—not after she had already failed. Charlotte had spent six months in captivity and during that time all kinds of unimaginable

horrors could have happened to Gabriella—
since she'd been left completely unprotected.

"She's pregnant, too," Charlotte said, as
with awe, she remembered her aunt's words
the first time they had talked. The phone connection hadn't been good, but she'd not mis-
interpreted that.

Aaron sighed. "Did you tell your father that
news?"

Charlotte tensed—not used to thinking of
the king as her father even though she'd known
for a few years now. Gabby had just discovered
her real parentage. So she was dealing with
all those conflicting emotions while she was
going to become a mother herself.

"I haven't told him yet," Charlotte admitted. "I'm concerned…"

"About how he will react?"

The king had never treated Gabby with the
respect she deserved. He'd never treated her
like what she was—an independent, modern
woman. "He already arranged for her to marry
another man."

"You don't think the baby she's carrying is
Prince Tonio Malamatos's?" Aaron asked, referring to Gabby's fiancé.

The prince had been waiting at the palace
when they arrived. As soon as the king had
notified him that the princess had been found,

he had come from his country with an entourage that included his ex-fiancée. When Charlotte had stepped off the plane, he'd mistaken her for Gabby and tried to embrace her. She shuddered as she remembered the man's clammy hands touching her arms, of his pasty cheek trying to press against hers.

Gabby never would have let that man touch her. Charlotte shook her head. "And neither do you. You know who the father is."

He expelled a ragged sigh. "Whit. If they'd been involved before she disappeared, it would explain why he was acting so strangely when you and Gabby went missing." Aaron had admitted that he'd been suspicious his old partner had been involved in their disappearances. "And why he was so anxious to bring her back once you told him where she was."

"I knew she had a crush on him," Charlotte admitted. "But I hadn't thought Whit would ever act on her vulnerability to him."

"Neither did I," Aaron admitted. "He's always been the professional, unemotional one."

Charlotte smiled as she thought of her sister. "Gabby has a way of getting to a person, of stealing her way into your heart."

But that hadn't worked with their real mother or with the queen. The person actually had to have a heart for Gabby to work her way inside. From everything Charlotte had heard about him, Whitaker Howell didn't have a heart either. But he had acted very worried about Gabriella and her safety.

Charlotte was also anxious about her sister. "I hope she's had access to medical care. And that she's not in need of it now."

"She's fine," Aaron said, referring back to Charlotte's most recent conversation with her aunt, who had called the palace at Whit's request. "Whit rescued her at the airport."

Charlotte breathed a soft sigh of relief. Whit had saved her. Just because he'd been doing his job? Or because he cared about Gabby?

In order to board the royal jet and return to St. Pierre, they would have to go back to the airport. And what if the gunmen were waiting there to try to grab Princess Gabriella again?

"We still should be there, too," Charlotte insisted. While the doctor had cleared her for flight and work, he'd cautioned her to take it easy. She'd been restrained to a bed for the past six months, so she'd lost some of her strength and stamina.

"The other jet has already taken off," Aaron said. "They're hours ahead of us and may have already landed."

"But they're not you and me," she pointed out. "And I'm not sure if Whit should trust anyone but you and me." Not with his life and certainly not with Gabby's.

Aaron snorted. "That shouldn't be a problem since Whit rarely trusts anyone."

"That's what's kept him alive for the past thirty years," Charlotte pointed out. But the problem was that he was traveling with a woman who trusted everyone, who always saw the good in people no matter what they'd done. Gabby would forgive Charlotte—eventually. But she wouldn't be able to do that unless Whit could keep her alive.

SIX MONTHS AGO Whit had been willing to let her marry another man, but today he had barely let the doctor speak to her before he'd ushered Dominic Delgado back to his Jeep. Dominic was an irrepressible flirt. Was Whit jealous?

Hope fluttered in her heart—and in her belly as the baby kicked with excitement. Could Whit care enough to feel jealousy?

He strode back through the doorway. "We have to leave now. The royal jet may have already landed."

So he hadn't been jealous at all. Just impatient to carry out his orders to bring her back to St. Pierre and her father. Disappointment quelled her flash of hope. But then she didn't want him to be jealous of her. Because if Prince Linus had been acting of his own accord and not his father's, then it must have been his jealousy that had cost Charlotte six months of her life.

She doubted he'd acted alone, though, because she doubted he'd cared enough to be jealous of her.

"You really want to bring me back to St. Pierre?" she asked. And her disappointment grew.

She had been right to leave him six months ago. Despite that night they'd shared, he hadn't cared anything for her—not enough to stop her from leaving. Not enough to stop her from marrying another man.

"You need to go back to St. Pierre," he stubbornly insisted. A muscle in his lean cheek, beneath the couple of days' worth of stubble and above his tightly clenched jaw, twitched.

"Why?" she asked. Nobody on St. Pierre genuinely cared for her—at least not enough to have ever been honest with her. "So my father can force me to marry Prince Tonio Malamatos?"

"That is not the reason why the king wants you home," Whit said.

She wasn't foolish enough to entertain any flutters of hope this time. Her question was more rhetorical than curious; despite the secrets he'd kept, she still knew her father well. Too well. "So he's broken that engagement for me, too?"

Good thing her question had been rhetorical because he didn't answer it. That muscle just twitched in his cheek again.

"Maybe Prince Tonio took my disappearance as a rejection and resumed his engagement to my cousin?" Actually Honora Del Cachon wasn't her cousin since Gabby wasn't really the queen's daughter. Like the queen, Honora had never liked Gabby, either. The night of the ball—when she'd been publicly humiliated—instead of blaming the king, Honora had glared at Gabby with such hatred that she shuddered even now, remembering it. "They could actually be married by now." And she fervently hoped that they were.

Whit shook his head. "Prince Malamatos refused to break your engagement until he had proof that you were dead."

"He waited for me?" she asked. Unlike Prince Linus, he didn't even know her. They had only met a few times over her lifetime, and had rarely spoken more than a couple of words to each other. So his loyalty wasn't personal.

Was her country that important to him?

Whit jerked his chin up and down in a rough nod. And for a second she wondered if he'd read her mind. But he probably only meant that the prince had waited for her.

"So he still intends to marry me when I return?" Panic rushed up on her now, so that she struggled to draw a deep breath. "And my father will expect me to obey his royal command and marry the prince."

"You can talk to him this time," Whit said, "instead of running away."

His words stung her pride. "You think I ran away six months ago?"

He gave a sharp nod. "I know that's what you did."

"I was threatened," she reminded him. Physically and emotionally. "And Charlotte thought I would be safer here." From both threats.

"Charlotte thought wrong."

"I was safe for six months," she said. And happy, despite feeling like a fool for giving her love to a man without a heart and for believing her family's lies. "I was safe until you came here."

He flinched but didn't deny that he might be responsible for the danger she'd stumbled into at the airport. "You're not safe anymore," he said. "We need to leave."

Distress attacked her again, making her

heart race and her stomach flip. "You don't care about me." She'd realized that long ago but it still hurt to know she'd given him so much and he'd given her so little.

She touched her belly. Actually he'd given her much more than he'd realized.

"Gabby," he said, his breath expelling in a ragged sigh of exasperation. Then he lifted his arms and reached for her, as if he intended to offer her comfort or reassurance.

But she held up a hand between them, holding him off. "And that's fine. I don't care that you don't care what'll happen to me on St. Pierre. But what about your baby? Don't you worry what will happen to him?"

There. She'd done it—she'd told him the truth. He was about to be a father.

But why would he care since he obviously didn't spare a thought for the baby's mother? She would try not to take it personally; perhaps Whit Howell cared about nothing and no one.

ALL THE BLOOD rushed from Whit's head, leaving him dizzy while heat rushed to his face. Sweat beaded on his brow. He brushed it away with a shaky hand. Maybe he should have let the doctor examine him, so he could have known for sure that he wasn't on the verge of having a stroke.

His heart raced, pounding fast and hard. And his lungs were too constricted for him to draw a deep breath. He had been in some of the most dangerous places and situations in the world, but he'd never felt such panic and fear before.

"Are you all right?" Gabby asked. Moments ago she'd pushed him away, but now she reached for him, her small hands grasping his forearms.

He nodded. But it was a lie. He wasn't all right. He was about to become a father—one of several things he'd sworn he would never be: a father, a husband, a besotted lover...

By leaving them, his mother had destroyed his father, sinking him deeper into the bottle, so that he hadn't been able to hold a job. Three years ago, when Whit had lost a job and struggled to get another, he'd felt like he was becoming his old man. And he had become more determined than ever to not even risk it. That was why he'd put up with the king and his asinine royal commands—because he hadn't wanted to lose another job. But now he risked losing so much more than just a job.

"Are you sure?" he asked.

She jerked her hands off his arms as if his

skin had burned her. Maybe it had. He felt like his face was on fire. And he still couldn't draw a deep breath.

But then she lifted her face toward his, and her big brown eyes were bright with indignation. "You know there was only you…"

His muscles tensed like they had that night when he'd realized she was a virgin, that despite all the media reports to the contrary, she had never been promiscuous. She had never been with another man before. Whit had tried to pull back, had tried to stop, but they'd both been too overcome with passion. And she'd urged him to take her—to take her innocence.

He'd done it because he'd wanted her so much and because he had really believed she'd wanted him. But the next morning when he'd returned to his room to change his clothes so that no one would realize that he'd spent the night with her, she had packed up and booked her flight to Paris. And he'd realized that he'd probably just been an act of rebellion for her, that she'd used him as revenge against her father.

"I know that I was the only one before you disappeared." He heard the Jeep's engine droning in the distance. "But you've been here six months…" Close to a man who had obviously fallen for her.

She lifted her hand, as if she intended to slap him, but then she drew in a breath and her control. And instead of touching him, she pressed her palm to her belly. "I am six months along. I was already pregnant when I came here."

He waited for more, waited for her to assure him that she'd slept with no other man but him. She offered no such assurances about her love life.

She only assured him, "This baby is yours."

But only the baby. She was not his. And she would never be.

If he brought her back to St. Pierre, her father might very well do as she feared; he might force her into marrying a strange prince. It was King St. Pierre's country, his rules. And he sure as hell wasn't going to let his princess become involved with a bodyguard.

"Where were you going?" he asked.

She blinked and then narrowed her eyes in confusion. "Six months ago?"

"No. Today," he clarified. "At the airport. If you had time to buy a ticket, where were you going to go?"

"The United States."

She'd be safer there than St. Pierre.

"Any state in particular?" he wondered.

She pressed her lips together, as if refusing

to answer him. Obviously she still intended to give him the slip, and she didn't want to make it easy for him to find her again.

"I'm not letting you out of my sight," he said. Especially not after what had happened at the airport. She could have been kidnapped or killed. And if he took his eyes off her for a moment, she would try to lose him again— leaving herself and their baby vulnerable.

Their baby?

He waited for the panic to surge back, but he could still breathe. His heart was beating— strong and steady—instead of the frantic pace it had when he'd first realized her baby was really his.

"Then why does it matter where I was going?" she asked with a slight shrug.

He fought an internal battle between following the rules and following his gut, between betraying friends and betraying her. His shoulder throbbed, as if his struggle had been physical as well as emotional. Or maybe it was infected. He really should have let Dr. Dominic examine it. But he ignored the pain and mimicked her shrug. "Because I want to know where we're going when we get to the airport."

She gasped in surprise over his admission. "You're not taking me to St. Pierre?"

He couldn't. Even before she'd told him

the baby was his, he doubted he could have brought her back to the people who'd betrayed her—who'd manipulated and lied to her for her entire life. She deserved better than that.

She also deserved better than him.

Maybe he should leave her here with the doctor and Lydia—people who were able to love and already loved her. That would be the right thing to do, but Whit rarely did what was right. Because even if it was right, it wasn't safe to leave her in a country where a man had already tried to abduct her and had nearly shot at her.

"No," he replied. "But we can't stay here, either."

"Because everyone knows where we are," she said, as if she'd read his mind again. But she continued to stare up at him, as if debating whether or not to trust him.

After discovering how many people had lied to her and for how long, she shouldn't trust anyone. Ever. Again.

He could figure out another place for them to go. During his years in the service, he had traveled so much that he had discovered some places where a man could hide. But a pregnant princess?

"I was going to Michigan," she said.

"Michigan? How did you know that's where

Charlotte was held for six months?" Had she already forgiven her sister and wanted to check on her?

Her brow furrowed with confusion. "I didn't. Where in Michigan was she held?"

"At a private psychiatric hospital called Serenity House." He nearly shuddered as he remembered the place that had been Charlotte's prison for six months and had nearly been where Whit had breathed his last.

She flinched with obvious regret and embarrassment. "I told Linus about Serenity House."

"How did you know about it?" he asked. She was inquisitive by nature; his men had told him that she'd often asked them about him. But he hadn't realized how knowledgeable she was.

"Someone told me about it," she replied, evasively avoiding his gaze.

Nothing had been less serene than a pregnant woman being held captive there for six months, restrained to a bed. It was also where Whit had been shot and would have been killed had it not been for Charlotte. He owed her his life. Could he keep her sister from her?

"Who did you talk to?" he asked, more worried than curious.

She shrugged. "Just somebody who lives near there."

"Did you meet her through Charlotte?"

She nodded. "Charlotte met her while she was still a U.S. Marshal. I think it was on her last assignment that they met."

And Whit's last assignment as Aaron's partner before they dissolved their business and their friendship. "Josie Jessup?"

Gabby shook her head. "That's not her name."

"It probably isn't now," he said. "But I bet it sure as hell was. I know who she is. And I've always known where she was in northern Michigan—not that damn far from Serenity House."

He had betrayed Aaron to make sure that Josie stayed safe, when he'd helped Charlotte fake his and Aaron's former client's death to put her in witness relocation. So to make sure she was safe, he'd found out where the U.S. Marshal had hidden her.

Gabby nipped at her bottom lip and then nodded. "Charlotte called her JJ."

"Charlotte shouldn't have told you anything about her." A man had been killed trying to find out where the woman, heiress to a media mogul's empire, was hiding. Whit had been forced to kill the man in order to save

Aaron's life and Josie's. His shoulder throbbed just thinking about the danger her knowledge put Gabriella in.

"Why the hell would Charlotte tell you where she is?" he asked. "Nobody should know." Maybe that was why the man at the airport had tried to grab Gabby—not because of who she was but of what she might know. It was information that someone had already killed for—information over which Whit had nearly died. Before he'd killed the man, the man had had gunmen try to kill him and Aaron. That was when Whit had taken the hit to the shoulder.

"She trusts her," Gabby explained. "And if anything happened to Charlotte, she trusted JJ and me to help each other."

While he'd been protecting her over three years ago, Whit had figured out that Josie Jessup was a smart, resourceful woman. What he hadn't realized was how smart and resourceful Gabriella St. Pierre was.

"We can't go there," he said.

"Of course not now," she agreed. "Charlotte would look for me there. That would have been a stupid place to hide." She shook her head, apparently disgusted with herself for considering it.

Gabby had yet to realize how intelligent and

capable she was. She must have read and believed too much of what was printed about her. Whit knew, intimately, how wrong the media had always been about her.

"If Charlotte was still missing, you would have been smart to go to Josie," he admitted.

With the former U.S. Marshal's help, Josie had learned how to disappear. And maybe that was what Gabby needed to do—not just for six months but for the rest of her life. It might be the only way she would escape her father's archaic insistence on ruling her life like he ruled his country—as a sole dictatorship.

"Why didn't you go to Josie earlier?" he asked, wondering why she hadn't the minute she'd discovered Charlotte had been keeping secrets from her.

Gabby glanced around that primitive hut. "I didn't want to leave here."

It obviously wasn't the conditions that had made her want to stay. So it was either the orphans, her aunt or Dr. Dominic. He hoped like hell it wasn't the doctor.

WHAT DID HE think about becoming a father?

Gabriella kept studying Whit's handsome face, but he revealed nothing of his feelings— after the initial shock. Maybe he was still in shock. But that could have been from the gunshot wound more than over what she'd told him.

"You really should have had Dominic examine you," she admonished him.

Whit shook his head. "I don't need a doctor. I need to get you out of here. Did you have all your stuff packed up?"

She nodded. Everything she needed was in her big backpack-style bag. She could no longer wear anything she'd brought with her six months ago. The clothes either didn't fit or hadn't stood up to the elements or how hard she had worked.

"Then we need to go," he said, heading toward the doorway.

But Gabriella stayed where she was, standing next to the bed, fingering the edge of the mosquito netting. "Can I really trust that you're not going to bring me back to St. Pierre?"

She had debated with herself before telling him about Michigan. While Charlotte hadn't trusted her with the secret that affected her own life, she had told her all about Josie Jessup and how Whit helping her relocate the woman had ruined his friendship with Aaron. So she knew he was very familiar with Josie's situation. Gabriella had no intention of putting JJ in danger. She'd only wanted to put herself and her unborn baby somewhere safe.

But apparently Michigan wasn't safe, either. But at least in Michigan, no one would make her marry someone she didn't know, let alone love.

He uttered a ragged sigh. "I'd like to think that you're wrong about your father—that he won't force you to marry Prince Malamatos…"

"You don't know my father like I do," she said.

After what she'd learned about her biological mother, she had to accept that she didn't know her father very well, either. Not that she didn't believe he would have cheated on the queen but she didn't believe he would have fallen for a con artist. Then again he hadn't fallen for the woman or he wouldn't have stayed with the queen. Or would he—just for the sake of propriety? Hell, the only thing she knew for certain was that nothing mattered to him as much as his country—certainly not either of his daughters.

Whit nodded his head in agreement. "That's why I can't risk it."

"Why do you care if I'm forced to marry the prince?" she asked.

He clenched his jaw again, so tightly that he had that muscle twitching in his cheek.

"Don't worry," she said. "I know you haven't suddenly developed feelings for me."

When he had so obviously not given a damn about her before now. "I know it must be because of the baby."

"I don't want another man claiming *my* child," Whit said, his voice gruff.

"So *you're* claiming your child?" she asked.

His chest lifted, pushing against his black T-shirt, as he drew in a deep breath. Then he nodded. "I believe you—that the baby's mine."

"But that doesn't mean you have to claim him," she pointed out, especially since he'd reacted to the news as if she'd shot him.

His already dark eyes darkened more with anger and pride. "You think I could walk away and pretend I don't have a child growing inside you?"

"So if I wasn't carrying your baby, you could walk away?" She needed to know that— needed to face the fact that it didn't matter that they were having a child together. They had no future together.

"I didn't say that."

"You didn't have to," she said. She grabbed up her bag from the bed and headed toward the doorway.

But he caught her arm, turning her back toward him.

"What?" she asked. "I thought you were in

such a hurry to leave that you couldn't even take a minute for the doctor to examine you."

"Forget the damn doctor!" he snapped.

"I think you mean that." Literally. That he wanted her to forget about Dominic. Did he think she'd been involved with the flirt?

"I spent six months thinking about you," he said, almost reluctantly as if the admission had been tortured from him, "thinking that you were dead and blaming myself for letting you go to Paris." His anger turned to anguish and guilt that twisted his handsome face into a grimace. "So, no, I couldn't walk away—even if you weren't carrying my baby."

Now the guilt was all hers. When she'd gone into hiding, she hadn't thought that anyone would miss her. Least of all Whitaker Howell.

"I'm sorry," she said. "I never meant for you to feel responsible."

Whit groaned, as if he were in pain. But was it physical or emotional? "I don't like feeling responsible. I don't like feeling...*anything*." He tugged her closer. "You make me feel all kinds of emotions I don't want to feel."

"I'm sorry," she said again, in a breathy whisper as attraction stole away her breath.

He was so close, with such an intense look of desire in his dark eyes. Then he was even closer, as he lowered his head to hers. His lips skimmed across hers, gently, only to return with hunger and passion.

Gabby reeled with the force of emotions so intense that her head grew light and dizzy. She clutched at his shoulders, holding tightly to him as her world spun out of control.

Six months had passed but she wanted him as desperately as she had the night of the ball, the night they'd conceived their child. Maybe she wanted him even more because now she knew what to expect.

Ecstasy.

But he tensed and stepped back from her. There was no desire on his face anymore—just shock and horror.

Then she heard it, too—the sound of engines, revving loudly as vehicles sped toward the compound. It wasn't just the doctor returning. There was more than one vehicle—more than one man.

They had waited too long. They'd been found, and if it were the gunmen from the airport coming, they had put the lives of everyone in the compound at risk.

Chapter Seven

Whit cursed. How had he let himself get so distracted? He would like to blame his gunshot wound. But he knew the real reason was Gabriella and all those feelings she made him feel that he didn't want to.

Like guilt. It pummeled him.

"If the guys from the airport found us, we can't let them hurt the children," Gabby said as she rushed toward that open doorway.

Whit stepped in front of her so she wouldn't run outside. "I won't."

She shook her head. "You can't protect them against all those men. I'll just let them take me. It's the only way to keep everyone safe."

She was serious—and more self-sacrificing than anyone he'd ever met. If he survived this, he might personally track down every paparazzi who'd called her a spoiled princess. A shallow ditz. They had no idea who Gabriella St. Pierre really was.

Whit wrapped his arm around her and rushed her toward the Jeep. He turned the key in the ignition and shifted into Drive. "We'll lead them away from here."

It was the only way to keep the children safe. They wouldn't destroy the compound looking for them—if they saw them leave.

"Hang on tight," he ordered her. If only the damn vehicle had seat belts…

And if only the road between the compound and town was more than a narrow path cut through the jungle…

He'd barely made it down that path when there had been no other vehicles on it. He really had no room to pass the Jeep and truck that were barreling down the track toward the compound. But he barreled ahead, and metal scraped metal, the driver's side of the Jeep scraping along the pickup.

Men filled the truck, inside the cab and standing in the box with long guns slung over their shoulders.

"Get down!" he shouted at Gabby.

"No!" she yelled back—even as bullets pinged against the metal of Whit's side of the vehicle. "They need to see me so that they know I'm not at the orphanage!"

As if to prove her point, she lifted her head higher and peered around him. And the windshield exploded as a bullet struck the glass. It continued into the rearview mirror, cracked the plastic and shattered the mirror.

"Get down!" he shouted again. But instead of waiting for her to comply, he reached across the console and pushed her lower.

Then he focused again on the road—just as a Jeep steered straight toward them. He clutched the wheel in tight fists, holding his own vehicle steady on the trail. And he trusted that the guy driving the other vehicle would give in to impulse—the impulse to jerk the wheel at the last moment.

Whit resisted his impulse even when Gabby lifted her head and screamed. But he didn't turn away. Metal ground against metal again, but the impact was lessened as the other driver twisted his wheel and turned the tires. Whit pressed hard on the accelerator, careening past, as the other vehicle bounced off trees and rolled back onto the trail—on its roof.

Shots rang out, continuing to break glass and glance off metal. Whit wouldn't have looked back even if the rearview mirror hadn't been broken. He kept speeding along the winding trail, widening the distance between him and the men who would have grabbed Gabby had they not escaped in time.

And, because his feelings for her had distracted him, they nearly hadn't escaped. For her sake, he could not succumb to emotion again.

GABBY COULDN'T STOP looking back—at the men who stood on the trail firing at them. And at the compound beyond the men. "Are you sure they won't go to the orphanage?"

"They saw you," he reminded her. "They know you're not there."

"But they might go to the compound," she said, her stomach churning with worry. "They might question Lydia to find out where we're going."

Whit snorted derisively. "They know damn well where we're going."

"The airport?"

"We have no other option," he pointed out. "We can't stay here."

"So once they get the Jeep moved and it is no longer blocking the trail, they'll come after us?" She had to know, had to make certain…

Whit nodded.

She exhaled a breath of relief. "So they won't go back to the compound." That was her most pressing concern—making sure the others were safe from the threat against her.

"Like I said, they know where we're going," Whit repeated. "Once they get that Jeep out of the way, they're going to be hurrying to catch up with us—not going back."

And Lydia would have heard the shots and the vehicles; she would have taken the children to the hiding place they'd built into the ground beneath the floors of one of the schoolrooms. They would be safe.

She wasn't so certain about Whit and her and their unborn child. While they'd lost the men—temporarily—he was driving so fast that it was possible they would crash, too, just as the men had.

"They want you," he continued. "You're the one the king will pay for…"

The king had already done it once—when he'd bought her mother's parental rights. It was no wonder so many others had tried to kidnap her over the years. They knew her father would pay their ransom.

But that was back when she had been blindly obedient. Now that she'd hidden from her father for six months, now that she'd become pregnant with the baby of a man who had nothing to offer him politically or monetarily…would he pay for her release? Or was she completely useless to him?

Whit's brow furrowed as he stared through the shattered windshield. "But if they wanted him to pay a ransom, why did they shoot so closely to you? Why risk it...?"

Her skin tingled with foreboding—the same way it had when she had found that crumpled letter under her pillow six months ago. Maybe they didn't want to kidnap her. Maybe they wanted to kill her as that note had threatened.

She braced one hand against the dashboard again and wrapped her other around the roll bar in the roof. She implored him, "Please, hurry."

Not that she needed to urge him to speed; he was probably already traveling too fast on dangerously curved, narrow roads.

"I'll protect you," he assured her.

She believed he meant it, but she wasn't necessarily convinced that he could. "I thought you were going to kill me when that vehicle was heading straight toward us..." And he hadn't backed down.

That was what his men had said about him; that he had never retreated from a fight—in battle or in the barracks. When he and Aaron Timmer had taken over as royal bodyguards, they had brought in their own men as backup. And she had quizzed all those men about their blond superior.

"I had it under control," he said. "You shouldn't have been scared."

She was afraid but not for herself; she was concerned for the child she carried.

And she was scared for the safety of the baby's father, as well.

SHE SHOULD NOT have trusted him. Whit had had no right to make her promises or offer her assurances that he had no idea if he would be able to carry out.

But he hated that her usually honey-toned complexion had gone pale with fear, her voice trembling with it. Her earlier scream echoed yet inside his head.

He didn't want her scared but he wanted her hurt even less. He had to protect her.

How? By taking her back to St. Pierre? He'd also promised that he wouldn't do that. But did he have a choice?

His shoulder was throbbing. His gun was out of bullets. He needed backup—backup he could trust: Aaron or Charlotte or any of the ex-military security guards he'd brought on board at the palace.

What had those armed men wanted with her? Were they working for Prince Linus's dad, or whoever the corrupt U.S. Marshal had been working for who had tried to find out where Josie was?

Were they intent on carrying out a kidnapping for ransom or a murder for hire?

Finally they neared the airport, and he slowed down to pull the Jeep off the road. Gabby reached across the console and grasped his arm. "Where are we going?"

Whit needed backup. But he didn't want her at the mercy of her father's royal commands. "We'll figure it out when we get inside. We're getting on whatever plane is taking off first."

He didn't give a damn where it was going. He just needed to get them the hell out of this place. After the earlier shooting, the airport should have been swarming with police. But he noticed no marked cars. No yellow caution tape…

Why hadn't the police come? Had they been called? Was there even a police force or military presence in this primitive country?

Gabby had a question of her own. "What about the royal jet?"

"We're not getting on it."

But the moment they stepped from the Jeep, men surrounded them. They weren't dressed in police or military uniforms but expensive suits. And like the men who'd stormed the compound, these guys, with jackets bulging over shoulder holsters, were armed.

And vaguely familiar. They had been royal

bodyguards. But he and Aaron had relegated them to perimeter palace guards when they'd taken over as co-heads of security for the king.

"Hey, Bruno. Cosmo," he awkwardly greeted the couple of guys whose names he hoped he correctly remembered. These men had been loyal to the king and to the former head of security, Zeke Rogers. Whit hadn't trusted that they would be as loyal to him and Aaron. It had actually been his call to move them out of the palace. Did they know that? Did they hold a grudge because of it?

"You kept us waiting," the one named Bruno remarked, his beady eyes narrowed even more with suspicion—especially as he studied the princess.

Did he suspect she was an imposter? Charlotte?

Or was he just as stunned as Whit had been to find her not only alive but pregnant?

"You should have given up on us and returned to St. Pierre," Whit advised them.

But no matter that Zeke was no longer their boss, they would remain loyal to the king and their country—probably out of respect and fear.

"We have orders," Cosmo added.

"Plans have changed," Whit said with the tone he used for giving orders in the field and on the job. And for the past several months, he had been giving these men their orders. To guard the gates of the palace. "It's too dangerous to take the princess back to St. Pierre."

Bruno pushed back his jacket and showed the Glock he carried inside the holster. "We have protection."

Whit didn't, and a strong foreboding warned him that he needed it. These men weren't acting like they did on St. Pierre. They weren't acting like he was their superior anymore. Had he been demoted? Zeke had been temporarily reinstated when he'd followed Aaron to Michigan to rescue Charlotte. But that reinstatement was only to have been temporary.

"Did you not hear me?" he asked, in his best no-nonsense boss tone. "I said that plans have changed. We are not going back to St. Pierre."

"We don't have to listen to you anymore," Cosmo said. "We take our orders from someone else now."

Damn. He had been demoted. Or fired.

They had protection, obviously. But he felt like he was the one who needed it now. Could he bluff them into thinking the gun he carried was loaded yet?

As Cosmo grabbed it from him, he realized it was too late. He shouldn't have trusted these men; he shouldn't have trusted anyone—just like Gabriella shouldn't have trusted him.

He couldn't keep any of his promises to her.

AARON'S HEART POUNDED slowly and heavily with dread. "Who did you send as Whit's backup?" he asked the king.

Rafael St. Pierre sat behind his desk in the darkly paneled den in his private wing of the palace. The past six months had added lines to the man's face and liberal streaks of gray to his thick hair. St. Pierre shrugged shoulders that had once been broad enough to carry the weight of his country, but in recent months they had begun to stoop with a burden too heavy—concern for his daughters' lives and safety. "I do not know the names of the men who went."

Neither did Aaron. And that worried him. "The men that Whit and I brought on are all still here in St. Pierre. They were told that Whit did not want them as backup."

"Then that is why they were not sent," the king replied.

Aaron shook his head. "Whit didn't know you were sending that jet after him. If he had known, he would have requested the men that he and I brought on to the security team."

"Are you certain?" the king asked. "I do not

believe Whitaker Howell is as loyal as you believe he is."

Just a week ago, Aaron would have agreed with the king. He'd thought Whit had betrayed him when he'd let Aaron believe that they had failed to protect their last client. Whit had actually helped Charlotte, in her previous position as a U.S. Marshal, fake the woman's death and relocate her. Neither of them had thought Aaron would be able to stand the client's dad's suffering as he mourned her; they'd worried that Aaron would give up the secret.

Maybe they had been right to worry. Because the secret he had now was on his lips, threatening to slip out. The king should be warned that Princess Gabriella was pregnant.

"If Whitaker Howell was loyal, he would not have gotten my daughter pregnant while she's engaged to another man!" the king shouted, anger exploding with his fist slamming against his desk.

Aaron didn't have much room to talk; he had gotten the king's other daughter pregnant. Charlotte hadn't been engaged, though.

"How—how did you hear that?" Aaron wondered. Charlotte hadn't told her father yet, and Aaron had managed to keep the secret until now. "Who—who told you?"

"A man who is actually loyal to me," King St. Pierre replied. Coldly.

He obviously wasn't too happy that Aaron had claimed Charlotte—as his fiancée—before the king had even claimed her as his illegitimate daughter and heir.

Aaron's head began to pound as realization dawned. "This isn't good…"

"No, it's not," the king agreed. "I trusted you and your partner. I believed the recommendations that Charlotte had given you both as exemplary chiefs of security. Yet you two were barely on the job a couple of months before my daughters both went missing."

"They were not hired to protect me and Gabby," Charlotte said as she joined them in the king's den. The guard at the door would have not dared to deny her admittance—even if it wasn't now common knowledge that she, too, was royalty, she could have easily overpowered the man.

She was that good. And Aaron was so proud that she was his.

"You're supposed to be resting," Aaron reminded her. For six months he had been so worried about her, but finding her hadn't changed his concern for her. If anything, given what she had endured and the baby she was carrying, he worried more.

She shook her head. "I spent nearly six months in bed. That's more rest than I can handle and retain my sanity."

The king rose from his chair, all concern now. "But you've been through a horrible ordeal—"

"That was not Aaron and Whit's fault," she said. "They were hired to protect *you*. I was supposed to protect Gabby and myself." Her voice cracked with fear and regret. "I am the one who failed."

Aaron reached for her, sliding his arm around her shoulders. She was the strongest woman he'd ever met—physically and emotionally. But she was hurting now—for her sister.

"What's not good?" she asked him.

And, just as they had all thought of him, Aaron couldn't lie. "Somehow King St. Pierre learned that Gabriella's pregnant."

She shook her head. "That's not possible. I didn't learn that until after I talked to Aunt Lydia, and I haven't told anyone but you."

"And I only told Whit," he assured her. "But the man who was shooting at her—he would have realized she was pregnant…"

The king slammed his fist into his desk again. "Are you saying that members of my own security team are trying to kill my daughter?"

Charlotte cursed with the vulgarity of a sailor rather than a princess. But then she had only just been identified as royalty. "This is why I wanted you to hire Whit and Aaron," she said. "Because all of your other security staff were mercenaries."

The king shrugged. "What is wrong with that? They are ex-soldiers, like Aaron and Whit."

"Mercenaries are not ex-soldiers," Aaron said. Because no one was ever really an ex-soldier. "They are still fighting but only now instead of fighting for their country or their honor, they fight for money."

"So they are easily bought," Charlotte explained. "And they are only loyal to the person who's paying them the most."

The king cursed now and dropped back into his chair as if he weighed far more than he did. His burden of concern and guilt was back—maybe even heavier than before.

"We need to call Whit," Charlotte said, "and warn him."

Aaron shook his head and lifted the phone he'd had clamped in his hand. "I've been trying. I can't get a call through to him."

"Call Lydia at the orphanage," Charlotte said. "Maybe they're still there."

"She won't pick up, either," Aaron said.

Both of the royals sucked in little gasps of air and fear.

"But remember the reception is bad down there," Aaron said, trying to offer them both comfort and hope even as his own heart continued to beat slowly and heavily with dread. "It doesn't mean that anything has happened."

Yet.

Would Whit realize before it was too late that the men who'd been sent as his backup were actually his greatest threat?

Chapter Eight

Gabby's heart pounded fast with fear—faster than it had even when Whit had been playing chicken with that other vehicle.

He was playing chicken again—resisting the armed men as they tried directing them through the airport toward the waiting plane. They pushed at him—with the gun barrel, and their hands, shoving him forward. He flinched as one of them slammed his palm into his shoulder.

Gabby bit her lip, so she wouldn't cry out with pain for him. He had already been hurting from earlier, and these men were using that weakness—exploiting his pain. She was too familiar with that cruel treatment—from the queen and her father.

"You kept us waiting long enough," Bruno remarked bitterly. "We have to go."

Gabby needed to leave now, too. With the men focused on Whit, she might have been able to escape. She could try to run back to the Jeep. And take it where? Leaving Whit behind?

Before she could make the decision, she was grabbed. A strong hand wrapped tightly around her arm, the pudgy fingers pinching her flesh. This time she cried out loud, more in surprise and protest than fear, though.

"Let her go!" Whit yelled, his voice so loud it went hoarse. He began to fight. Forgetting or ignoring his injury, he swung his fist into one man's jaw—knocking him out as easily as he had the one she'd shot earlier that day.

He had saved her then. But there were too many of them for him to be able to save her now. A gun barrel was pressed tight to his back, between his shoulder blades.

It was almost as if Gabby could feel it, too. The bite of steel, the fear of taking a breath since it might be her last. Or Whit's last. She didn't want him to move, but he continued to struggle.

"Don't," she whispered, imploring him with her eyes to stop fighting. These men had claimed they no longer took orders from Whit. Had her father fired him? Or were they actually working for someone else?

"I will shoot you," Cosmo warned him.

"Is that one of your orders?" Whit asked. "Did the king tell you to shoot me?"

Gabby took that breath now—in a gasp of shock. She had long ago realized that her father was not the nicest man. He was selfish and manipulative. But was he a killer? Would he have Whit murdered?

She wouldn't put it past him—if he'd learned that his bodyguard had impregnated his daughter and potentially foiled his plans for a royal merger. He would never approve of her being with a man who offered *him* nothing—no money or political influence.

"Stop!" she said, shouting even though she barely raised her voice. Instead she used her father's imperious tone—the one with which he issued commands that no one dared to disobey.

And the men actually stopped pushing them forward—toward that damn plane. It was a royal jet sitting on the primitive tarmac, but it wasn't her father's personal, far more luxurious jet. So he had not made the trip to retrieve her himself. Had he missed her at all the past six months?

"As Princess of St. Pierre, I am ordering you to release Mr. Howell," she commanded. Relieved that she had kept her nerves and adrenaline from cracking her voice, she expelled a soft sigh.

Whit jerked free of Cosmo while two other men helped up the one he'd knocked to the ground. Bruno groaned, too disoriented to avenge himself on the man who'd struck him. Taking advantage of Bruno's weakness, Whit reached for the man's weapon.

But before he could grab it, a shot was fired—into the ceiling, like she had fired earlier. The bullet ricocheted off the metal and sent people running for safety, screaming.

Gabriella covered her stomach with her palms even though she knew her hands weren't enough to protect her child. She had to use her brains instead.

"Stop!" she yelled again. This time her voice did crack—with a show of weakness and fear. And men like these, men like her father, always took advantage of fear and weakness to assume control.

But perhaps she was the only one who'd noticed her vulnerability because the men again paused in their scuffle. Even Whit this time… as if he was afraid she might be caught in the crossfire or the ricochet if more bullets were fired.

"I will not be using the royal jet today," she

imperiously told them, "so you need to take it back to St. Pierre."

The other men turned toward Cosmo, as if to verify her claim. He shook his head. "We have orders that supersede yours, Your Majesty."

Damn her father! The king was the only one whose orders would supersede the orders of the princess of St. Pierre. Was he so desperate to force her into marriage with a stranger that he would risk her safety? That he would authorize the violent treatment of Whit?

Her stomach lurched, and so did her baby, with the fear that her father had learned of her pregnancy. And his anger had overwhelmed whatever capacity he'd had for human kindness.

With a quick glance at his watch, Cosmo said, "We need to board the plane now."

Her father must have been keeping them to a tight timetable. And if she kept them waiting any longer, they would get more impatient and probably violent.

For fear that Whit or someone else might be struck if more shots were fired in the airport, she allowed herself to be ushered outside to the waiting plane. Whit fell into step beside her, occasionally lurching ahead of her as one of the men pushed him.

She wanted to yell again, but he gave a barely perceptible shake of his head. He must have already decided not to fight her father's orders. He had decided the same thing six months ago when he'd waved her off to meet with a designer for the gown in which she would marry another man. Even though she hadn't really gone to meet that designer and she'd had no intention of buying a wedding gown, Whit had not known that. He just hadn't cared...

She'd been foolish to think that he ever might be jealous of her. It didn't matter to him that she was carrying his child. That had not changed the fact that he had no feelings for her—despite what he'd said back at the hut about her making him feel.

And that kiss...

Her lips still tingled with the sensation of his mouth pressed to hers. And that kiss brought back memories of how they'd made their baby—of how those kisses had led to caresses and making love.

No. She'd been the only one making love. She was beginning to think, as those who knew Whitaker Howell best had warned her, that he wasn't capable of feeling anything. They had been referring to his seeming inability to feel fear no matter how dangerous the situation. But if a man couldn't feel fear, then he probably couldn't feel love, either. She should have realized that then, but she'd been so hopeful and naive.

What a difference six months had made in her life. Back then she'd been a silly girl building foolish fantasies around a man who would never be hers. Who would probably never be anybody's...

And now she was a woman about to become a mother, being forced to return to a life she'd never wanted and over which she had no control. Her father was a difficult and selfish man, but was he really so intent on getting his own way that he would risk Whit's life and hers?

At the bottom of the steps up into the plane, she hesitated. If she ran now, would they shoot her? Or just chase her down and force her onto the plane?

And what would become of Whit if he tried to help her? Would he even try?

WHIT'S GUTS TWISTED into a tight knot of anger and frustration as he stared down into Gabriella's beautiful face. Her skin was pale, her eyes wide and dark with fear. She stared up at him expectantly, as if waiting for him to save her.

He had to help her. He shouldn't have made those promises—to protect her and to not bring her back to St. Pierre, but he had. And he needed to figure out how to keep them.

But he was outgunned and outmanned. And if he struggled again, the men might leave him behind—alive or dead.

And then Gabriella would be alone with them.

He lifted his chin to break free of the hold of her gaze. And he turned away from her, heading up the stairs first. He wanted to be aboard—needed to get on that damn flight with her. He couldn't let her go back to St. Pierre alone.

He glanced over his shoulder. A couple of the men flanked her, each grabbing an arm to guide her—hell, to nearly lift her—up the stairs to the plane. He clamped his arms to his sides, so that he wouldn't reach back—so that he wouldn't pull her from their grasp. They better not be squeezing her arms, better not be pinching or bruising her.

He hated them touching her. Hated more that they might be hurting her.

He turned away to step through the door to the plane. As he was shoved down the aisle, he passed a man already sprawled in one of the seats. The guy's shoulder was bandaged, and his arm was in a sling. A big bruise was turning from red to purple along his swollen jaw.

This was the man who had tried to abduct Gabby earlier—when she'd been alone. He must have arrived at the airport the same time Whit had. Hell, maybe he'd even beaten him there. Gabby had figured that the man being there was just a coincidence—that he had seen her alone and unprotected and decided to take advantage of the opportunity. Whit didn't believe in coincidence. He'd figured the man might have followed him from Michigan.

But what if this man had already known where Whit was going? Where Gabby was?

The guy was obviously affiliated with the top guards from the previous royal security regime. As an independent security contractor or a mercenary? He could have been working for anyone. The person who'd left her the threatening note. Or Prince Linus's father. Or whoever wanted to find Gabby's new friend, JJ…

Behind him he heard Gabby's gasp as she, too, recognized the man. Then her gasp turned to a moan. Whit whirled back just in time to see her crumple into a heap in the aisle. He tried to rush toward her, but the guys holding him pushed him down into a seat.

"Princess!" yelled one of the men, as if his shout would bring her back around.

But she wasn't unconscious. Instead she

was clutching her stomach. "I'm going to be sick," she warned them. "I need to use the bathroom."

Cosmo helped her to her feet. Then he guided her down the aisle toward the restroom in the back. As she passed Whit, he fisted his hand at his side, so that he wouldn't reach for her. But he didn't need to touch her to assure himself she was all right.

She shot him a pointed glance. She knew they were in danger, and she was working on a way to get herself and their child the hell out of it. The media couldn't have been more wrong about her.

But no matter how smart she was, she was six months pregnant and as outnumbered and weaponless as he was. Whit had to help her and not just because it was his duty. And not just because it was his baby she carried...

"I need to call the king," he said, slowly reaching for his phone. But his fingers no more than closed around it before one of the men knocked it from his hand. As soon as it hit the aisle, the man slammed his foot down onto it. "I need to tell him that the princess is too sick to travel."

As if on cue—and maybe his words had been exactly that—retching sounds drifted down the aisle from the restroom. This wasn't the king's royal jet; this was another in the fleet, used more for cargo than for passengers. The seats were not as luxurious nor the bathroom as large. She had to be uncomfortable in the tiny space. Hopefully she wasn't really sick; hopefully she was just faking in order to keep the plane on the ground.

"She is too far along in her pregnancy to fly," Whit said, as he stood up. "We can't take off."

"We have orders," Cosmo said. He moved away from the bathroom door—as if unable to tolerate the noises Gabriella was making inside the tiny room. He walked up to Whit, clasped his wounded shoulder and shoved him back down into the seat. "We're taking off…"

Whit ignored the pain coursing down his arm and fisted his tingling fingers. "You can't—"

They weren't listening to him or Gabby. One of the men sealed the outside door shut and then knocked on the cockpit door.

"…now," Cosmo finished with a triumphant grin. "We're taking off *now.*"

"If the king knew she was sick," Whit persisted, "he wouldn't want her flying."

The engines fired up, causing the plane to vibrate. Then it moved as it began to taxi down the runway. "You can't take off now!" Whit shouted. "She's not even buckled in."

She would be tossed around in that tiny space—with no seat belt and nothing to protect her and her baby from getting hurt. It would be even worse than her ride in the Jeep because it would be thousands of feet in the air with the risk of turbulence.

He tried to rise up again, but another man shoved him into the seat. Whit couldn't reach her—couldn't help her.

Cosmo snorted. "If she's going to get sick, better she be sick in there than out here." He shuddered, and his throat moved, as if he were struggling with sickness of his own.

"She could be hurt," Whit said. "The king will not approve of that."

Emotionally hurting his daughter hadn't bothered the king. But when the man had seen that trashed hotel suite in Paris and he'd thought she might be physically hurt, Rafael St. Pierre had been distraught. He hadn't feigned his worry for her during the six months she'd been missing.

"So what's he going to do?" Cosmo asked. "Fire us again?"

"He didn't fire you," Whit replied. "You were just reassigned." But maybe he shouldn't remind them that he was the one responsible for their demotion. Then again, maybe goading them would make them rethink their loyalty to the king. "You were assigned to the same job a trained guard dog can do."

As a fist slammed into his jaw, he regretted his words. Bruno shook his hand and cursed. Then he grabbed at the seats around him as the plane's tires lifted from the airstrip.

Whit's back pressed against the seat they'd pushed him into, but he tried to stand up again. He had to get to Gabby—had to make sure she was all right. "If she gets hurt, the king might do more than fire you. He wouldn't have ordered his own daughter harmed!"

"No, he wouldn't have," Cosmo agreed. "You keep making the mistake of assuming our orders are coming from the king."

Oh, God! The royal security force had been compromised and the royal jet hijacked.

Whit doubted he had to worry about their bringing them back to St. Pierre. He had to worry about their bringing them anywhere.

Alive.

GABRIELLA'S HEART POUNDED fast and furiously, and it wasn't just because she was a somewhat nervous flyer. She had her hands braced against opposite walls of the tiny bathroom.

And her ear pressed to the door, she heard everything being said between the men.

They weren't acting on her father's orders. She figured that might have been the case when she'd boarded and recognized the man she had shot. The fact that he'd already been aboard the plane meant that he was working with the men from her father's old security team. And she doubted her father would have approved that man nearly shooting her. Because he would have if not for Whit knocking him out.

She had suspected then how much danger she and Whit and their baby were in. So she had feigned the fainting and sickness to get away from them.

Having her suspicions confirmed actually produced a flash of relief before panic overwhelmed her. These men didn't work for her father.

So who did they work for?

The person who'd left that note threatening her life? Or Linus's father, determined to carry out his creepy plot? Or were they working for themselves, having come up with their own retirement plan: ransom?

If that was their plan, they might let her live—at least until they got money from her father. But what about Whit? They had no reason to keep him alive.

She had been waiting for the royal bodyguard to help her. But he was the one who needed her help. She had only just realized that when she heard him goad the men.

"You can't fire those guns on a plane. One stray bullet and you could bring it down."

Were they already going to execute him?

She eased open the door slightly and peered through the crack. Whit was in the aisle, pushing against the men standing between him and the cockpit.

"Then we'll make sure all of them hit you," Bruno replied, lifting his weapon to point the barrel right at Whit's chest.

The men were so focused on him that they didn't notice as Gabby eased out the door. She stepped into the aisle and snuck toward the back of the plane—to the cargo hold.

Assess the situation...

Charlotte's words echoed inside Gabby's head. Her former bodyguard had used this very scenario as an example in order to teach Gabriella how to protect herself during a plane hijacking.

Gabby remembered giggling at the time, totally amused that her bodyguard had been so paranoid that she'd thought something that farfetched could happen aboard the St. Pierre royal jet. But now that the scenario had become a reality, Gabriella was frantically trying to recall the advice Charlotte had offered. She wanted that voice inside her head, but all she could hear was Whit's.

"Bullets have a tendency to go right through me," he cockily replied and rolled his wounded shoulder as if to prove his point.

Damn him and his macho bravado...

If he got the renegade guards to fire, he would not only die but he would risk the whole plane going down. Gabby needed to find a parachute. Because sometimes the most effective mode of self-preservation was escape...

She pushed open the door to the cargo hold, hoping she would find at least a parachute—hopefully more. But as she slipped into the hold, a commotion erupted inside the plane. Flesh connected with flesh as men threw punches and kicks.

Gabby flinched with every grunt and groan—as if the blows were hitting her. And inside her belly, the baby flipped and kicked. Whit wasn't the only fighter. Gabby could fight, too, and not just how Charlotte had taught her. She could fight now as a mother fighting to protect her child.

And her child's father.

She only hoped she found something to help Whit before it was too late and the men had already killed him.

Chapter Nine

Pain radiated from Whit's shoulder throughout his body—to every place a blow had connected. But he had landed more blows than he'd received. He had even knocked out a couple of the men.

But then Bruno lifted his gun again, this time swinging the handle toward Whit's head. He ducked and the blow glanced off his wounded shoulder.

He groaned so loudly that his throat burned from the force of it. Pain coursed through him, but rage followed it, chasing away the pain. Blind with anger, Whit reached out and jerked the weapon from Bruno's beefy hand.

Before he could slide his finger onto the trigger, barrels pointed at him and triggers cocked with ominous clicks.

"Drop it!" Cosmo ordered.

Whit shook his head. "You're not the one giving orders here. Who is?"

"You're not going to find out," Cosmo said. "You're going to be dead long before we land."

Even though he'd grabbed a weapon, there were still too many fighting him. He might not make it off this plane, but he had to know about Gabby. "What about the princess? Does the person giving orders want her alive or dead?"

"What does it matter to you?" Cosmo asked. His eyes narrowed and he nodded. "Ever since you started at the palace, she was always asking everybody about you and following you around, mooning over you. So is that baby she's carrying yours?"

Whit clenched his jaw, grinding his teeth together with frustration that he couldn't claim his baby. Doing so might risk the child's safety and Gabby's. The last man who had thought he'd kidnapped her, but had abducted Charlotte instead, had wanted to get her pregnant with his own child. Even though Prince Linus was in custody, he was still a wealthy man; he or his father could have paid these guys to abduct the right woman this time.

Cosmo took Whit's silence as affirmation and shook his head in mock sympathy. "Too bad you'll never get to see it being born."

Because they were going to kill Whit or because they were going to kill Gabby, too?

"Shoot the damn gun!" The order echoed inside the cabin, but it was a female voice that uttered it. A sweet, strong voice—Gabby's. She stood near the entrance to the cargo hold.

When he'd heard her stop her fake retching, he'd figured she was going to sneak out of the bathroom soon. So he'd provided a distraction for her. That was why he'd started swinging despite being outmatched. He had wanted to distract the other men, so they wouldn't notice her. Apparently she'd gone from the bathroom to the cargo hold. Looking for an escape or a weapon?

"Whit," she said, making it clear her order was for him, "trust me—shoot the gun!"

"What the hell?" Cosmo whirled toward her with his gun drawn.

And Whit couldn't trust that the other man wouldn't fire. So he did. He lifted his gun and fired a bullet through the roof of the cabin.

The other men cursed as the plane dropped, losing altitude fast. Whit leapt over them, heading toward Gabby. He had fired the gun because he'd figured out her plan; he only hoped it wouldn't get them killed.

"You TRUSTED me," she said, surprised that he had actually fired. And afraid that he had. She swung a parachute pack toward him.

But the plane lurched and Whit nearly missed it. And he narrowly missed the hands reaching for him as he grabbed up the pack and ran into the cargo hold with her. He shoved the door shut and jammed something against it. "There better be another way out," he said. "And fast…"

She pointed toward the parachute and turned her back toward him to show she'd already put on hers. His hands caught the straps, pulling them tight, as he double-checked all the lines and cords.

"Are you sure parachuting will be safe for the baby?" he asked.

"Getting shot will be a hell of a lot less safe," she pointed out, as the men fired now, shooting their guns into the hold.

Whit pulled his pack on and adjusted the straps, pulling them taut. His shoulder wound was again oozing blood, which trickled down his arm in rivulets. The parachute straps were going to stress the wound even more. She should have considered that, should have thought of something else. But he agreed, "We have no other option now."

"Is the plane going down?" she asked, as it continued to lose altitude.

"Probably crash landing. We have to get out soon." He hurried over to the luggage door to the outside and struggled with its latch. "I think I can get it open…"

She hadn't thought out any of her plan. Maybe Whit shouldn't have trusted her. Maybe he shouldn't have fired. But if he hadn't, he would probably already be dead. While she hadn't been with him these past six months, at least he had been alive. At least she'd had hope that he might one day become the man her naive heart had believed he was. But if he was dead…

Then Gabby had no hope.

"Come here." He held out his hand. "We have to be ready to jump when I open this luggage hatch."

She'd faked getting sick earlier but her stomach lurched now, threatening to revolt for real. She hadn't thought this plan out well—hadn't considered all the consequences. She had parachuted before—with Charlotte, who had set up a scenario eerily similar to this so that Gabby would be prepared if her plane were ever hijacked.

Gabriella had loved the freedom of parachuting, the weightlessness of floating on air. But she hadn't been pregnant then. She'd had no one else to worry about except herself.

The door to the cabin vibrated as if one

of the men were kicking it or slamming his shoulder into it.

"We have to do this now," Whit said. "We're dead for sure if we don't."

And possibly dead if they did…

He opened the door to the outside, causing the plane to buck as if they were trying to ride a crazed bull. Whit grabbed her hand and tugged her out with him—sending them both hurtling through air.

If only there had been time to tell him…

Tell him what?

That she loved him? Six months ago she'd thought she was falling for him, but she hadn't even known him. She'd been attracted to his masculine beauty and his aura of strength and mystery. And the fact that he hadn't seemed to give a damn about anything or anyone…

She'd wished she could have been like that—that the queen's rejections and cruelty hadn't mattered to her. But she'd thought the woman was her mother, so she'd been devastated and desperate to please—so desperate that she'd let her father bully her.

And she'd let people lie to her—because she'd felt the secrets and hadn't probed deeper. She hadn't demanded the truth because she'd been afraid to hear it. She hadn't thought herself strong enough to handle it.

But she was a hell of a lot stronger than she'd realized. She was strong enough to jump out of a crashing plane.

But she wasn't strong enough to tell Whit that she had nearly fallen for him...before she'd begun to fall with him...

All she could do was hold tightly to his hand and hope she didn't lose him—hope that she didn't lose her baby or her life.

HE WAS LOSING her. His arms ached, his shoulder burning, as he struggled against the straps, tugging off the chutes before they pulled them both under water. Part of the chute, the part they'd slipped on with the straps, was a life jacket. But it was thin and barely enough to keep them above the surface of the choppy water. They had landed in the ocean—with no land in sight.

And only God knew what waiting, beneath the surface, to devour them...

After the struggle on the plane, his wound had re-opened. Was his blood baiting the water? Maybe he should leave her before he drew sharks to them. He tried to peer beneath the surface but the setting sun reflected off the water, blinding him. Making the water look as if it were all blood...

"Gabby!"

She squeezed his fingers. She had been clinging to his hand since they'd leaped out of the dropping plane. "I'm here..." But she sounded sleepy, groggy, as if she were so exhausted that she was about to pass out.

Whit recognized the signs in her voice because he felt them in his own body. He pushed his legs to kick, to keep them above the waves that kept lifting them only to drop them again. Water slapped his face, as if trying to keep him awake. He needed that because the life jacket wasn't enough to keep his head above water, but only enough to keep them from dropping to the bottom of the sea. It would make their bodies easier to find when they were dead...

"Are you all right?" he asked.

"Yes," she replied.

"And the baby?"

She smiled. "He's fine. Kicking as if he's trying to swim, too."

"He? You keep calling the baby a boy," he realized. "Do you know...?"

She shook her head now, her wet hair slapping across the surface of the sea. "I don't know for certain. It's just a feeling I have."

A gut instinct. Whit understood that, but unfortunately the gut instinct he had now was bad. If only he'd had more time before they'd jumped, he could have tried to find supplies to

take along. But he might have lost them anyway, like he had the gun he'd shoved into the
back of his jeans. It had fallen out when they'd
hit the water and sunk like a rock.

"I can't believe," she said, "that we survived…"

His gut tightened with dread as he worried
that she spoke too soon. "We survived the
plane crash," he agreed.

But would they survive a night in the sea?

"Did it crash?" she asked, leaning back to
stare up at the sky. It was nearly black now, the
last of the light glowing on the surface of the
water. There were no lights in the sky.

"Not near us…" He had worried that it might
go down as they were jumping and take them
both out as it crashed. While he and Gabby
had been drifting on air, he'd caught glimpses
of the plane as it spiraled forward and down-
ward. With its speed, it had gone a good distance ahead of where they landed in the water.

But given the waves and tides, some of the
wreckage could drift back toward them.

"But you think it crashed?" she persisted.
Maybe she was so concerned because she
needed a distraction, or needed to make sure
that the men weren't going to come after
them again. But knowing her, she was probably worried about the well-being of the men

who would have killed them with no hesitation or remorse.

"I don't know." And truthfully he didn't. He'd been in worse situations and had had pilots pull up the throttle and safely land the aircraft. "I don't know who the pilot was. The king's pilot could have handled the changes in cabin pressure. He could have kept it in the air and landed somewhere." But he knew it hadn't been that pilot, or the plane wouldn't have been waiting at the airport as long as the men had complained they'd been waiting.

She expelled a breath of relief. "Yes, they might be okay, then..."

She really was too good—too perfect—to be real. He must have conjured her up from those old, half-forgotten fairy tales. He wasn't as perfect as she was. Hell, he wasn't even close to perfect or forgiving or caring. So he had to ask for clarification, "You're worried about men who would have had no qualms over killing us?"

He tensed as he glimpsed something dark in the water, moving just beneath the surface. Beneath them. Had the sharks begun to circle? They, too, would have no qualms over killing them.

"When I told you to shoot," she said, in a voice hoarse with remembered panic and with regret and probably dehydration, too, "I—I didn't realize that the plane might crash…"

"It doesn't matter if it did," Whit said. "You were in danger." And still was, with no land in sight, and the waves getting rougher. Their bodies bobbed as the waves lifted and then dropped them—almost as if the water toyed with them, giving them hope only to dash it away. He held more tightly to her hand, his own going numb with cold and the effort to keep hanging on. "You had to save yourself."

"I—I don't know for certain that they would have killed me," she said, her teeth chattering slightly.

With the sun no longer warming the water, it had quickly gone cold. Flesh-numbingly cold.

"You think they only intended to kidnap you?" They hadn't seemed concerned enough about her safety, and they knew the king well enough to know that he would have paid no money without proof of life.

"I don't know what they intended to do with me," she said with a shaky sigh. "But I do know what they intended to do with you. They were definitely going to kill you, Whit."

He shivered but not just with the cold. He'd had close scrapes over the years, probably more than his share even for a marine and a bodyguard. But he'd always managed to figure his own way out. Until now…

"So you weren't worried about yourself," he said. "You were worried about me." He wasn't used to people worrying about him. His mother certainly hadn't when she'd packed up her stuff and left him with his father. Back when they'd been friends and partners Aaron had worried, but then Aaron worried about everyone.

"They had no reason to keep you alive," she said, "and more reasons to want you dead."

"With a bum shoulder and no weapon, I didn't pose much of a threat to them," he pointed out.

She chuckled. "But you're Whitaker Howell. You're a legend for the feats you've pulled off in battle, for the people you've protected as a bodyguard. They would see you as quite the threat."

"Or quite the pain in the ass," he said. "And it probably didn't help that I brought in my own men to take their jobs when Aaron and I were hired as co-chiefs of royal security."

She must have shaken her head because a wet piece of her hair slapped against his arm. Her hair and her skin was so cold. He wanted to put his arms around her and warm her up. But then he risked them both slipping under water.

"So you parachuted out of a plane to save me," he mused. "And here I was the one who promised to protect you." A promise he was still struggling to keep, as he tried to keep them both afloat.

Water splashed her face, and she sucked in a breath and coughed. And as she panicked, her head slipped beneath the choppy surface. Whit panicked, too, but he didn't let go of her hand. And with his other arm, his injured arm, he dragged her back up. She sputtered and coughed again, expelling salty water from her constricted lungs.

"Are you all right?" he asked.

"Y-yes," she stammered. "And you are my protector."

With the right resources, he was a damn good bodyguard. He could protect anyone from armed gunmen, from bombs, from fires...

But he had no idea the threats that lurked beneath the surface of the water. And no way of protecting her from them. Or from the water itself as it chilled their skin and blood, threatening hypothermia.

He'd been told it was a peaceful death. It was how his father had gone, too drunk to get the key in the door—he'd died on his front porch during the dead of winter—while Whit had been in the sweltering heat in a desert on the other side of the world. He wasn't going out like his old man. "We need to stay awake," he said. "We need to stay alert…"

"To what?"

He wouldn't tell her his fear that there was something circling them. He focused instead on offering her hope. "If the plane did go down, someone would have noticed it on radar. They might send out boats or helicopters to search for survivors."

Given that he'd seen no sign of land when they'd dropped into the sea, a search party was their only chance.

"You think help's coming?" she asked.

"Yes, if not strangers—then Aaron and Charlotte will send someone or come themselves."

"But how will they know where to look for us?" she asked. "How will they know to look for us—that we're still alive?"

"Aaron will know," Whit said. "Just like he knew that Charlotte was alive." But that was because he loved the woman, because he had a bond with her. Or it was because the man always looked for the best in a situation.

Whit should have known that Gabriella was

alive the past six months. But he'd never been as hopeful or optimistic as Aaron. He always expected the worst; there was less risk of getting disappointed that way.

"He loves her?" Gabby asked.

"Yes."

She fell silent, just floating in the dark. So he prodded her, "We need to keep talking…"

"About—about what?"

He chuckled. "Your nickname is Gabby. You can't think of anything to talk about?"

"I—I only chatter when I'm nervous."

If there was ever a time to be nervous, it was now—adrift at sea at night. "Tell me about the orphans," he said.

She wasn't gabby. She was eloquent, as she told him beautiful stories of the children's triumph over all the tragedies of their lives. She talked until her teeth chattered too much for her to get the words out. "Your turn," she told him.

"I'd rather hear you…" And he would. He loved the sound of her voice, the way it slipped into his ear and into his heart.

"If you want to distract me from how cold I am," she said, "I'm better at listening." Something else about her the paparazzi had gotten completely wrong.

"You're going to make a great mom," he said. If he could keep her and their baby alive...

She sniffled, either from the cold or from emotion. "I don't know about that. I didn't exactly have a loving mother growing up. Or biologically. What kind of mother gives up her baby for money?"

"At least she had a reason," he said. And he talked. He told her about his mom and his dad. Maybe he told her the stories to warn her that he wouldn't be a good husband or father. Or maybe he just told her to keep her awake.

But her grasp on his hand loosened, and her fingers slipped free of his. He couldn't lose her now—he couldn't lose her and the child she carried. Since he was a kid, he had sworn he would never have a family—that he wouldn't put himself through the risk of disappointment and pain.

But now his greater fear was that he was going to lose the chance at having one. Even if a search party was dispatched, the wreckage of the plane was nowhere near them. They would probably be presumed dead. And soon that might be true...

THE KING'S DEN WAS FULL of people now. Because she was so beloved, nearly every member of the household staff had gathered to hear word of Gabriella's well-being. Her fiancé was also there, along with his ex-fiancée, who claimed she had come out of friendship to him and relation to Gabby. She was the queen's cousin, which made her no relation to Gabby. But Charlotte wasn't about to explain that situation—or even talk to her.

Nor was she going to talk to the father and brother of Gabby's ex-fiancé, who claimed they had also come out of concern. She was surprised they'd had the audacity to show, after what Prince Linus Demetrios had done. But maybe they wanted to watch King St. Pierre suffer, as they were bound to suffer with the prince in prison now. They probably blamed the whole thing on the king, for breaking that engagement in the first place.

Charlotte suspected that he was blaming himself, too. Even with all the people gathered around, he looked so alone, removed from the others as he sat behind his ornate desk on a chair that was too modern to resemble a throne. But it was still one regardless of the design.

The man was used to being in control—not just of his own life but of every life in St. Pierre. He was helpless now. Charlotte's heart shifted, as if opening slightly to him. He had made mistakes. So many mistakes...

But so had she.

Would Gabby ever forgive either of them? Or had she died hating them both?

A man strode into the den, and all the chatter in the room ceased. All heads turned to him, as if he were the king about to make a royal decree.

But Charlotte knew him best, so she knew what he was going to say before he even opened his mouth. The anguish and hopelessness was in his blue eyes, dimming the brightness that Charlotte loved so much. The regret was in the tight line of his mouth, and the anger and frustration in the hard set of his strong jaw.

Guilt attacked her first. It was all her fault—her stupid plan that had put them all at risk. But even before the plan, she had hurt Aaron. She'd cost him his friendship with the man who'd been as close to him as a brother. While she'd spent the past three years getting to know her sister, he had lost those three years of friendship; he and Whit had been estranged. Because of her...

They had only just repaired that friendship to lose it again. Forever, this time...

Aaron cleared his throat, as if choking back emotion. But it was clear and steady as he spoke, "The plane went down. A search party went out to the wreckage, but there were no survivors."

Now the grief hit her. Hard. Grabbing her heart and squeezing it in a tight fist.

"She's dead," a woman's voice murmured into the eerie silence after Aaron's pronouncement.

"We don't know that," he corrected her. "Her body wasn't found."

"But you said no survivors..." The woman was Honora Del Cachon, the ex-fiancée of Prince Malamatos.

"From the wreckage of the plane," Aaron said. He looked at Charlotte now, his gaze holding hers. His eyes had brightened again—not as much as they usually were when he looked at her. But he wasn't entirely without hope. "But I'm not sure Princess Gabriella went down with the plane."

"Why not?" Charlotte asked the question now. She had to know if he was only trying to make her feel better or if she had a real reason to hope.

"Because Whit's body wasn't found either..."

She wanted to be as optimistic as the man she loved. But she wasn't like him and Gabriella—who always found the good in everything. She was more like Whitaker Howell, more realist than idealist. "But if they parachuted out before the plane crashed…"

She had an idea of where it had gone down because she'd been with Aaron and the king when they'd been told it had gone off radar. Aaron had gone out to the area where it had crashed, to look for survivors and verify that it had been one of the royal jets. She'd wanted to go along, but he'd insisted she stay behind— probably because he'd worried that she might lose the baby if she had proof that her sister was dead.

That was probably why he was offering false hope now. She couldn't take it.

"…they landed in the middle of the sea," she said, "with no land in sight. No help…"

The only boats to pass through the area, where they would have had to jump to escape before the plane crashed, were drug runners, arms dealers and other pirates.

"And they would have been in the water all night," she added. "With as cold as it gets when the sun goes down, there is no way they could have survived."

She hated that the brightness dimmed again in her fiancé's eyes. But she couldn't cling to a lie. She had to face the reality that her sister and Whit were gone.

Forever…

Chapter Ten

"Stop!" she ordered him. "Put me down."

But Whit ignored her protest and tightened his arms around her. The waves slapped at his legs as he fought his way from the surf to the beach. He staggered onto the sand.

"I can walk," she said, but she wasn't certain if she spoke the truth. After hours in the water, her legs were so heavy and weak that they had folded beneath her when she'd tried to stand in the shallows.

That was when Whit had grabbed her up his arms, arms that had strained against the waves to swim them to shore. Land. They had reached land.

Or was it just a mirage on the endless water? Or a dream? She had nearly fallen asleep several times. Her life jacket had been fairly useless, so her head would have slipped beneath the surface if not for Whit holding her above water.

How had he stayed so strong? So alert? Amazed by the man's power, she stared up into his handsome face.

Despite the cold they'd endured all night, sweat beaded on his forehead and above his tense mouth. His arms shook from exertion. He was more than exhausted. He was wounded, blood streaking down his arm from his shoulder. It was a miracle the blood hadn't drawn sharks to attack them.

"Put me down," she ordered again.

He stumbled as his feet sank in the sand, but he didn't drop her. That promise he'd made to protect her was one he obviously intended to keep—no matter what it cost him. His health. His strength. His life.

He trudged across the sand, which gave way to a slate patio and stairs leading up from the beach to a glass-and-stone house perched on a hill high above the water. "This island is inhabited," he said.

When they'd first noticed it, it had seemed little more than a clump of trees in the distance. As they'd swum toward it, the island had gotten bigger but not much. It was just a small stretch of sand, a rocky cliff and a clump of trees. They'd worried that it would be uninhabited. But maybe this was just a tiny peninsula of a bigger island.

"You're not going to carry me up all those steps." Gabby fought harder, so that she finally wriggled free of his grasp and slid down his body. Her legs, numb with cold and exhaustion, trembled and threatened to cave again before finally holding her weight.

Fortunately there was a railing beside the stairs, which Gabby climbed like a rope to help her to the top of the steep hill. She gasped at the view at the summit. It was just the hill and the house and the beach below that. The other side dropped off even more steeply to rocks and water. It was no peninsula of a larger island or continent.

"This is someone's private retreat," she said as Whit joined her at the top.

He was battered and bruised from his battle with the men aboard the plane. And his skin was flushed either from the sun or with a fever.

After those interminable hours in the darkness, she welcomed the warmth of the sun. But maybe the shock of going from the frigid water to the sunlight was too much for Whit. Could his body handle any more trauma?

He nodded. "There's a helicopter pad over there." He gestured with a jerk of his chin as if his arms were too tired to lift.

She followed his gesture to where the trees

had been cleared on the other side of the hill from the house. "No helicopter. So nobody's home?"

Whit walked around—or more accurately—staggered and peered between the trees down all sides of the hill. "There's a dock on this side of the island." This time he managed to point but not with the arm of which the shoulder was wounded. "But no boat."

Panic struck Gabby. She'd been so hopeful that this place would prove their salvation. But with no means of escaping if someone were to follow them here, they were trapped.

"So there's nothing but the house?" she asked.

IT WAS ONE hell of a house. Nowhere near as grand as the palace, of course, but Whit preferred its simple lines. Made of glass and stone, it became part of the landscape, bringing the outside in as sunshine poured through the windows, warming the slate floor beneath their feet.

The door hadn't been locked. There would have been no point—probably nobody knew where the place was but the owner. Maybe that was a good thing; maybe a bad thing...

It depended on who owned the place and for what reason he required such seclusion. This part of the world wasn't known for its tourism, more for its guns and drugs and lawlessness.

Whit had checked every room to make sure the place was empty before he'd left Gabby inside alone. Even though he'd only been gone minutes, he expected to find her asleep when he stepped back inside, but she was in the kitchen, flitting around like a bedraggled butterfly.

"You got the power on," she said with a sigh of relief. "There must be a generator?"

He nodded as he took a seat on one of the stools at the granite kitchen island. Like the rest of the house, the kitchen was all slate and glass. "And enough gas to keep it running for a while."

"There's a lot of food, too," she said. "Dry goods and canned fruit and vegetables and juices. We'll have enough to eat until someone finds us."

Whit nodded, hoping that the right people would find them and not the ones they'd just jumped out of a plane to escape. Or worse yet, the person who had given those men their orders. And what exactly had those orders been? To kidnap the princess? Or kill her?

"Nobody will look for us here," she said, as if she'd read his mind and wanted to set it at ease. "They probably think we're dead."

"Maybe they're right." His head pounded

and his shoulder throbbed. And his stomach rumbled with a hunger more intense than he ever remembered, even when he'd been a kid and his dad had forgotten to buy groceries. Or he'd spent the money on liquor instead of food. "I feel like hell."

She pushed a plate of food at him. She'd done something with canned chicken and pineapple, and as he ate it, he became certain he wasn't dead. Because this felt too much like heaven, with her as an angel, and he'd never imagined he'd wind up *there*.

As soon as he finished eating, she was at his side, helping him up from the stool. His legs shook from the effort. God, he was so damned tired. He'd never been so tired—not even during his first deployment with those bombs exploding all night every night...

"You need to rest," she said, guiding him down the hall toward the bedrooms.

He shook his head. "I have to keep watch. Make certain no one takes us by surprise..."

She chuckled and assured him, "We'll hear them coming..."

He listened and could hear nothing but the waves crashing against the shore below. He never wanted to hear water again—never wanted to be near it—not after all those endless hours they'd spent drifting in it.

"Go to sleep," she said, gently pushing him down onto the bed.

He caught her hand, needing to keep track of her. He couldn't lose her again—not like he had six months ago—when he'd thought he'd lost her forever—not like when she'd slipped away from him at sea.

"Don't go," he said. "Don't leave…"

The words brought him back to his childhood—to what he'd said when his mother had packed her bags and walked out with them—leaving him behind. She hadn't paid any attention to what he'd said, to what he'd wanted or needed.

But Gabby settled onto the bed beside him. And her cool hand stroked across his brow. "You're so hot. I wish Dominic was here."

Jealousy flashed through him that she wanted another man…when he wanted only her.

"You need a doctor," she said.

He shook his head. "No. I only need you…"

I ONLY NEED *YOU*.

He'd been delirious with a fever when he'd said those words. He probably hadn't even known who she was. But still she couldn't get that line out of her head. And when she slept… she dreamed it was true.

That he really needed her. That he loved her as she had never been loved. Now she was back to being the young girl weaving foolish fantasies.

It was time to wake up. The sun was beating hard through the windows, warming the room and her body. She squinted even before she opened her eyes. But the sun wasn't shining in her face.

A shadow covered her—the broad-shouldered shadow of a man. Backlit by sunshine, she couldn't see more than the shadow at first. So she screamed.

He leaned back, and the sun bathed his face and glinted in his golden hair. "It's all right," he said. "You're safe. It's just me."

Then she wasn't safe at all. Not emotionally. He'd gotten to her again—gotten into her heart. The night they'd spent on the water, endlessly talking, she'd learned more about him than any of his friends could have told her. She wondered if even Aaron knew exactly how Whit had grown up. Alone.

He had probably thought they were going to die. That had to be the reason why he'd told her all that he had. All his pain and disappointments...

Or he'd hoped that if they lived, she would know better than to expect a happily-ever-after from him. He didn't believe they existed. And with good reason.

She shouldn't believe in them, either. But even though she hadn't experienced them personally, she'd seen them—when she'd visited boarding school friends who had found happiness with men who loved them.

But maybe Whit couldn't love—because he didn't know how. And she wasn't certain that was something that could be taught. No one had taught her to love, but it hadn't stopped her from falling for this man. With resignation and wonder, she murmured, "It's just you..."

His lips twitched into a slight grin at her remark. His hair was damp and water glistened on his bare shoulders and chest.

"You took a shower," she said, around the lump of desire that had risen up to choke her. A droplet trickled down his chest, and she had to fight to resist the urge to lick it away.

"I needed to—to wake up," he said. "Looks like you did, too. Your hair's still damp." He put his hand in it, running his fingers through her hair—which was probably still tangled despite her efforts to comb through the thick mess.

Grateful for the generator running the pump, she'd taken a shower and put her clothes in the mini–washing machine she'd found. But she hadn't found any clothes to wear while she slept. So the only thing between her and him was a thin sheet and the towel draped low around his lean hips.

"How long was I asleep?" he asked. "Days?"

He touched his jaw—which was clean-shaven now. He must have found a razor because when she'd checked on him last he'd had a lot of dark blond beard growing on his jaw. Even asleep, he'd been tense—his jaw clenched. "Weeks?"

She had lost track of time, thinking of him. Dreaming of him. But since her hair was still damp, she hadn't been asleep that long.

"A day and a half," she said. "And you probably still need more rest."

"No." He shook his head and leaned close again. His dark eyes were intense as he met her gaze. "That's not what I need."

Her pulse started racing, her blood pumping fast and hard through her veins. She had to ask, "What do you need?"

"You," he said. "Only you…"

She must have been sleeping yet—caught so deeply in the dream that it felt real. Like his lips skimming across hers, she could feel the warm soft brush. And then his tongue slid inside her mouth—in and out. Her skin tingled with desire and then with his touch, as his hands skimmed over her naked shoulders. He moved his lips across her cheek, to her neck.

She shivered now.

"Are you cold?" he asked.

She shook her head. Her skin was catching fire with the intensity of the passion she felt for him. That desire chased away the last chill from their night in the cold sea. "No…"

He kissed one of her shoulders and then her collarbone and the slope of her breast. Then he pushed down the sheet, skimming his hands over her breasts. But he stopped with his palms on her belly. "Can we do this?" he asked.

"We jumped out of an airplane," she reminded him. And during the whole parachute trip down to the water, the baby had kicked—as if with excitement. He was probably already as fearless as his father. Panic flickered at the thought, at how she would have to worry about him, like she worried about Whit.

"I doubt a doctor would have recommended that." Whit tensed, his eyes widening with shock.

"Are you all right?" she asked. "Are you hurt?"

She knew he had needed more rest and a doctor to examine his wound. But it looked better now, the edges of skin melding together around the puckered hole where the bullet had entered his body.

"I—I'm fine," he said. "And so's he. He's kicking." He stared down at her belly, obviously awed that there was life inside her. "He feels strong."

She smiled at the fatherly pride he was already showing. "He is."

"You really think the baby's a boy?" he asked, almost hopefully.

Did all men want sons? She knew her father certainly had. Perhaps that was why he hadn't claimed Charlotte because she hadn't been the male heir he'd really wanted. And then by the time Gabriella had come along, he'd wanted an heir so desperately that he'd taken what he'd gotten despite his disappointment. Now he intended to barter her for a man, for a son-in-law, to help him rule his country.

No matter how much she had fallen for Whit, her father would never approve him as her husband. He had no family. No country. Nothing her father could take in trade. Gabriella only wanted one thing—from both men. Love.

If she couldn't get it for herself, perhaps she could for her child. "I don't know for certain he's a boy. The orphanage had no access to an ultrasound to prove it."

"What about other prenatal care?" he asked.

"Dominic took care of me."

That muscle twitched in his cheek again. "You should have found me, should have told me, and given me the chance to take care of you."

"I didn't know that you'd want to," she admitted. "In fact I was pretty convinced that you wouldn't want to."

He uttered a ragged sigh. "If you had asked me if I wanted to become a father, I would have told you no."

She flinched as his brutal honesty struck her hard. "I'm sorry…"

"But now that it's going to happen," he said, "I'll deal with it. I'll figure out how to be a good parent."

"Figure out?"

He shrugged. "I told you—that night on the water—I didn't have good examples."

"I know," she murmured. The stories had been more about warning her than sharing with her.

"My mom took off when I was little," he reminded her, "and my dad cared more about drinking than raising a kid."

As it had when he had first told her about his upbringing, sympathy for him clutched her heart. "I'm sorry…"

"You didn't have any better examples," he reminded her—again with the brutal honesty. "Aren't you scared?"

"Terrified," she admitted.

"You don't need to be," he assured her, stroking a fingertip along her cheek. "You will be a wonderful mother."

He had told her that before—on the water. And she hadn't asked then what she should have. "How do you know?"

"Because you care about people," he said. "You're not selfish…"

"Like my father?" Would she be as controlling with her kid as he'd been with her?

"He wasn't responsible for those men on the plane," Whit said in his defense. "They weren't following *his* orders."

So he wasn't a monster, just a bully. "I know," she said. "That's why I figured out we needed to jump."

"You took a huge risk…"

Her heart flipped with fear even just remembering. So many things could have gone wrong.

"Take a risk on me," he said, lowering his head to hers. He kissed her again—with passion and desire.

He had to be real. This couldn't be a dream.

But what did Whit want her to take a risk on? Loving him?

It was too late. She'd already fallen in love with him. Six months ago. And so many things had gone wrong...

Except for conceiving their child. And except for making love with him. That hadn't felt wrong. That had felt as right as what he was doing to her now.

He made love to her mouth and then he made love to her body, kissing every inch of her. He teased her breasts with his tongue, tracing a nipple with his tongue before tugging the taut point between his lips.

She cried out as pressure built inside her body. She arched her hips up, silently begging for the release she knew he could give her. And he teased her with his fingers, sliding them gently in and out of her. Then he pressed his finger against the point where the pressure had built. And she came, screaming his name.

He moved away, dropping onto the mattress next to her. Sweat beaded on his brow and his upper lip, and the muscle twitched in his cheek.

"Are you all right?" she asked, concern chasing away the pleasure afterglow.

He groaned. "I will be. I just need a minute."

His body betrayed him. He'd lost his towel, so she saw the evidence of his desire.

"Make love to me," she urged him.

"I don't want to hurt you," he said, and he pressed a hand to her stomach. "Or him…"

"We're fine," she assured him. But she wasn't completely fine because the pressure was building again. "But I need you. I need to feel you inside me." And because she was afraid that he would hold back, she took the initiative.

She straddled his lean hips and eased herself down onto his pulsing erection. She moaned as he sank deeper and deeper.

He clutched her hips and lifted her up. But instead of pulling her off, he slid her back down. Up and down. He thrust inside her. And as he thrust, he arched up from the mattress. He kissed her, imitating with his tongue what he was doing to her body.

The intensity of the pressure built and built…until he reached between them. He pushed against her with his thumb, and she came again.

He thrust once more and uttered a guttural groan, as he filled her with his pleasure.

Tears stung her eyes from the intimacy of their joined bodies and mutual ecstasy. Her heart swelled with emotion, with love. She had never felt anything as intense until she'd felt her baby's first little flutter of movement.

She loved Whit with the same intensity that she loved their baby. And she wanted to share that love with him.

But when she opened her mouth to speak, he pressed his fingers against her lips. "Listen," he said.

And she waited for him to speak, hoping that he was going to declare his feelings. Hoping that he loved her, too.

But he said nothing. Instead he cocked his head and narrowed his eyes. Then he asked, "Do you hear that?"

"What?"

"I think it's a helicopter."

"You think the owner is coming back?" Heat rushed to her face over the embarrassment of the homeowner finding them naked in his bed.

"I hope so," Whit said, but his body had tensed again. And that muscle was twitching in his cheek.

"But you don't think it is?"

He shrugged. "It could be. But my gut's telling me that it's not."

"You think they found us?" She had almost

hoped they would believe she was dead again and not look for her.

"I think we're about to find out."

Chapter Eleven

Earlier, when he'd awakened from his long sleep, Whit had checked out the house again. Instead of just searching rooms, he'd searched every drawer and cupboard. And he'd found something the owner had left behind that he'd worried might prove useful.

A Glock.

He pressed it into Gabby's hand. "You take this," he insisted. "And stay out of sight."

They had dressed quickly, in clothes that were still damp from the washer, and Whit had retrieved the gun, before they'd slipped out of one of the many sliding doors of the house. That first day, he had found a little storm shelter close to the outbuilding that held the generator. But the cavelike hole was so small that they both barely fit inside its stone walls. That didn't matter, though, since Whit wasn't staying. He moved toward the cement steps that led back to the trapdoor like entrance.

Gabby clutched at his arm with fingers that trembled. "Don't leave."

"You'll be safe here," he assured her.

"Then you will be, too," she said. "Stay here. Stay out of sight with me."

He shook his head. "That might be help arriving on that helicopter." It had probably already landed, but the generator was too close to the shelter and too loud for them to hear over the droning engine. "It could be Aaron and Charlotte."

He doubted it, though. If the plane had crashed, there probably would have been no survivors—no one to share the news that they'd parachuted out. But before the plane had gone down, one of them might have called his boss—the one really giving the orders. That person might be aware that they'd gotten off before the crash.

And he might have launched a search party to make sure they hadn't—or wouldn't—survive.

"I'll go with you," Gabby said, anxious to see her sister now. How like Gabby it was to have already forgiven Charlotte for the secrets she'd kept…

"We don't know for sure who it is," he pointed out. Even if it was the homeowner, Whit wanted to meet him alone first and gauge the person's trustworthiness before he revealed the princess of St. Pierre. "So I need to check it out first."

"Then take the gun with you," she said, pressing the Glock back into his hand, "in case it isn't help arriving."

"If it isn't, you may need the gun," he said. "It didn't take me long to find the shelter— they could find it, too." He intended to cover that door in the ground, though, with branches and leaves.

"You'll need the gun more than I will, then," she argued, "since you'll be encountering them first."

The woman was infuriating and beautiful and generous and loving. And Whit should tell her all those things. He had wanted to tell her earlier. Those words and so many others had been on the tip of his tongue, but then he'd heard the helicopter in the distance. And he had known that this was neither the time nor the place for him to share his feelings.

And if that wasn't help arriving, there may never be a time and place for him to tell her that he was falling in love with her.

"You need the gun," he said, "to protect yourself and our baby."

She drew in a shuddery breath and finally stopped trying to push the gun on him. He knew that she wouldn't have kept it for herself, but she wanted to protect their baby.

So did Whit. He would make sure that she wouldn't need to use that gun. He would protect her and their baby no matter the cost— even if he had to give up his life for theirs.

GABBY FLINCHED AS the baby kicked her ribs— hard. He was kicking her, too, like she was kicking herself for keeping the gun. She should have insisted Whit take it with him. She shouldn't have let him leave the shelter with no protection.

Maybe she should sneak out and see who had arrived, see if Whit would need the gun. She climbed the stairs toward the trapdoor, and standing beneath it, she listened intently. But all she could hear was the generator and the sound of her own furiously beating heart.

The baby kicked again, and she pressed her free hand against her belly—trying to soothe him even as her own nerves frayed. If she really was safe where she was, why hadn't Whit taken the gun?

Could she risk her child's life to save his father?

Whit would never forgive her if she ignored his wishes and risked her own safety and their baby's. But perhaps even being where she was would endanger them. If someone found them, inside the shelter, they would be trapped. She could get off a few shots, might hit one or two of them. But what if there were more than a couple of them?

No. She couldn't stay in the shelter. It wouldn't be safe if she were to be discovered hiding in the cavelike hole because there was only one way out—through the trapdoor. She tried to lift it now, but it was heavy.

She managed to raise it an inch and dirt and grass rushed in through the narrow space. Choking on dust, she dropped it back down. Whit had covered it, had tried to camouflage it.

His friends claimed that his instincts were legendary and had saved more than one life during their deployments. For him to hide her as he had, his instincts must have been telling him that it wasn't help arriving.

They'd jumped out of a plane that had probably crashed. Why would anyone suspect they lived? Charlotte and Aaron were too realistic to believe in miracles. The only person who might know they'd survived was the one who'd hired the men, if the pilot or one of them had called him before the crash.

And if it was one of them, then Whit was disposable. He was only in the way of what—

ever plan that person had for her. Kidnapping or killing…

Whit, no doubt, had a plan to protect her and their baby. Like covering the hole to the shelter so no one would find her. But she worried that in order to carry out his plan he would have to sacrifice too much.

Perhaps his life…

WHIT HAD WALKED BACK through the living-room slider before passing through the house to the front door. That way, hopefully, the person wouldn't realize he had been outside.

He drew in a deep breath and opened it to a man he wasn't surprised to see. The guy was bald with heavy black brows and more scars than Whit and far fewer morals. Zeke Rogers had accepted his demotion with even less grace than the other men. He had to be the one who'd been giving them orders—since that had been his job before Whit and Aaron had taken it from him.

Whit was glad that he'd given Gabby the gun because Zeke was smart. He would find her eventually—unless Whit could outsmart him.

"You're like a cat with nine lives, huh?" Zeke remarked almost idly. He obviously wasn't surprised to see Whit either, or to find him alive and on this island. "You just keep coming back from the dead."

"I haven't died once," Whit corrected him. Yet. He had a feeling this man intended to change that.

"I heard about the bullet you took in Michigan," Zeke said. "That's why the king had me resume my duties at the palace, as his royal guard."

"We agreed that would be best," Whit admitted, "while Aaron and I concentrated our efforts on finding Charlotte and Princess Gabriella. But Charlotte has been found." And Aaron should have resumed his duties as chief of security, dismissing Zeke again.

"The princess has been, too," Zeke claimed.

Whit's stomach muscles tightened as if he'd taken a blow. But he resisted the urge to glance toward the shelter and make sure Gabby wasn't being dragged from her hiding place. Zeke could have other men searching the island. One of them could have found her.

But she was a fighter. He doubted she would have been taken without firing at least one shot, which he would have heard even over the drone of the generator engine.

Denying Zeke's claim, Whit shook his head. "She's gone…"

"The king sent you to retrieve her from

Charlotte's aunt's orphanage." The man had obviously been briefed—either by the king or by someone else. "You had her. You two were on the royal jet together before it went down."

"It went down?"

Zeke nodded, but his face displayed no emotion. He didn't give a damn that men he'd worked with had probably lost their lives. Probably while they'd been trying to carry out his orders...

"Were there any survivors?" Whit wondered.

Zeke shook his head now. "Just you and the princess."

So he had been in contact with the men on the plane—obviously right up until the moment it went down. "Why would you think that?" Whit asked, trying to get the man to make the admission. Not that it mattered if he confessed...

Whit was convinced Zeke Rogers wasn't there to help him or Gabby.

"Well, obviously you're alive."

Whit nodded. "Obviously."

"You and the princess parachuted out of the plane."

There was no point in denying what Zeke had apparently been told. "That's true."

"You weren't easy to track down," Zeke

said, resentment flashing in his beady eyes. "I had to talk to some parachuting experts and some experts on ocean currents to figure out where the hell you might have washed up."

Whit had a feeling the man had been hoping to find bodies rather than survivors. "It really was nice of you to go to all the trouble to rescue me."

"I'm not here to rescue you," the man ominously corrected him.

Whit lifted his arms, ignoring the twinge in his shoulder, and gestured around the empty house. "Well, I'm the only one here."

Zeke chuckled. "Where are you hiding the princess?"

Whit forced a ragged sigh of regret and resignation. "She didn't make it."

"She wasn't on that plane when it went down," Zeke insisted. "She parachuted off with you."

"Yes, but that was much too dangerous in her condition. There were complications..." He paused, as if choked up.

"With her pregnancy?" Zeke asked.

He was too superstitious to lie about that, not wanting to tempt fate. So he just shook his head. "She was weak and the water was just too damn cold. We were in the sea overnight." He shuddered, for real, as he remembered the frigid water and how it had numbed his muscles and burned his skin. How the hell had they survived?

He shuddered again. "She didn't make it…"

Zeke narrowed his eyes. His voice terse with skepticism, he asked, "You just let her die?"

"I couldn't do anything to help her." He really hadn't. She'd fought for herself and for their child.

Zeke snorted, derisively. "So you're not the hero everyone thinks you are."

Whit shrugged. "I never claimed I was a hero."

"You haven't needed to—all those men you hired that you served with—they make the claims for you. That's why the king made you his right-hand man." Along with the resentment, there was hatred.

"You'll probably get that job back now," Whit said, "since I failed to protect what matters most to the king." No matter how callously he'd treated his daughter, the man did love her. He had been so genuinely distraught over her disappearance that he had to care. And as Whit had learned for himself, the woman was damn hard not to love. He'd fought his feelings, but it was one of the first battles he'd ever lost.

"I thought she mattered to you, too," Zeke remarked.

"Why would you think that?"

"Heard she was following you around like a puppy before she disappeared," he said. And now there was jealousy. He was too old for Gabby. But hell, at thirty, with the life he'd lived, so was Whit. "And nobody missed the way you looked at her, too."

"She's a beautiful woman."

Zeke arched one of those creepily bushy brows.

"Was," he corrected himself, silently cursing the slip. "She was a beautiful woman."

"She was pregnant, too," Zeke said.

"Did you have a bug on that plane?" he wondered. The men wouldn't have had much time to tell him everything. But the first man, the one Gabby had shot, would have had time to inform him of the princess's pregnancy.

"I'm just thorough," Zeke said. "I believe in doing a job well."

Whit couldn't argue with him. While Zeke had protected the king, the monarch had not been harmed. But Charlotte hadn't trusted the former mercenary. She had suspected that his loyalty was for sale to the highest bidder, and that if someone paid him more than the king, that Zeke Rogers would do whatever they wanted. The man had no morals, no principles and no conscience. Obviously Charlotte had been right.

"Maybe you should have been sent to retrieve the princess then," Whit said.

"I have been," Zeke retorted. "Now."

The skin on the nape of Whit's neck tingled with foreboding. "It's too bad that you're too late."

"It would be if I actually believed you." The man pushed past Whit and strode purposely through the house, searching every room.

Feigning shock and offense, he asked, "You don't take me at my word?"

Zeke snorted in reply and just continued to search.

Whit followed, breathing a sigh of relief that he'd stripped the bed in the room in which he'd awakened. It didn't look as though anyone had slept in it. It didn't look as though anyone had slept in Gabby's bed, either. The sheets were tangled and damp.

But Zeke didn't seem to notice. He checked under the bed and the closet and continued through the house.

"Satisfied?" Whit asked. "She's not here."

"I won't believe Princess Gabby is gone,"

Zeke replied, "until I see her dead body." And if her body wasn't dead, did he intend to make it that way?

"You're not going to find it in the house." Whit managed to furrow his brow with feigned confusion. "I've been checking the beach..."

"Waiting for her to wash up?"

He flinched at the agonizing thought.

"Give up trying to sell me on this line of bullshit, Howell," Zeke said. "There's no way in hell you lost her in the ocean."

He nearly had—when her hand had slipped out of his. But he'd caught her before she'd slipped beneath the water.

"We didn't land near each other," Whit lied. "By the time I swam toward where she'd landed, the chute lines had pulled her under. She was gone..."

Zeke pulled his gun from the holster beneath his jacket. "You better hope you're telling the truth, Howell, because if I find her..."

"You're going to kill her?"

Those bushy brows arched in question. "Why would that matter to you—if she's really already dead?"

"Just didn't think the king would order his daughter killed," Whit said. "So who are you working for now?" He knew Zeke didn't intend to let him live, so he might actually tell him the truth.

"Someone who wants the princess to never return to St. Pierre."

"Who?" Whit persisted.

Zeke taunted him, "If she's really dead, what does it matter?"

Whit couldn't say it—couldn't bring himself to utter the lie. Before today he had never been superstitious, but he couldn't risk it now—that saying she was dead wouldn't somehow make it come true.

"I want to know who you're working for," Whit persisted.

"Why?" Zeke asked. "It's not like you're going to need a job anytime soon."

Whit shrugged. "You don't know that. The king is not going to be happy with me for not bringing the princess home."

"The king won't fire you," Zeke assured him. "Because he won't need to. I'll fire you for him." And he lifted the gun and pulled the trigger.

Chapter Twelve

The sound of the gunshot echoed off the hill-top. Gabby felt the vibration of it in the sliding door against which she leaned, trying to see inside. But Whit had pulled the drapes across it, blinding her to what was going on inside the house.

Who had gotten off the helicopter? And had Whit just calmly let them inside the house to shoot him?

Her heart pounded furiously and so loudly she could hear it ringing in her ears. Or was that just the echo of the shot yet?

The wind picked up, whipping her hair around her face. And she realized what the noise really was: the sound of another helicopter.

Was it backup for the first? More of the men from the plane?

She clutched the gun she held. Should she storm inside the house? Or should she run to the helicopter in the hopes that it might actually be someone to help? Her head pounded with indecision and fear. Her instincts had her wanting to storm inside the house—wanting to protect Whit.

So she followed her instincts and pushed open the patio door. She listened but heard no voices, no sound above the pounding of the helicopter blades as it approached that small pad on the other side of the house. She drew in a deep breath and lifted the gun before stepping inside.

Glass crunched beneath her feet as she crept across the living room. The coffee table top had shattered, leaving only the brass frame. And that had been twisted. Chairs had toppled onto the slate flooring.

There had been a struggle. But there was no body left behind to tell her who had won or who had lost. Where was Whit? And with whom had he struggled?

He had rested for a day, but he hadn't completely recovered from their overnight in the sea or his gunshot wound. As she studied the mess, she noticed the dark liquid spattered across the glass fragments and the slate. She crouched down, as far as her burgeoning belly allowed, and reached a trembling finger toward the spill. Then she lifted her hand and

analyzed the stain smeared across her fingertip. A bright red stain.

Had Whit's wound re-opened or did he have
a new one?

Tears stung her eyes. Tears of regret and
guilt and anguish. She shouldn't have waited
so long before coming out of the shelter. She
should have followed him right back inside the
house. What kind of mother was she going to
be for her baby if she'd done nothing while his
father had been harmed?

Where was Whit? How badly was he hurt?

She wasn't just concerned that her baby
might have lost her father. She was concerned
that she might have lost the man she loved…
and before she'd even had a chance to tell him
how she felt.

WHIT HAD HAD to get Zeke outside—because
he'd noticed the shadow outside the slider. And
he'd known that Gabby had been too worried
to stay where he'd put her. She'd been worried
about him—when she should have been more
concerned about herself and their child.

She'd done the same thing at the orphanage—making sure the men had seen her, so
that they would leave her aunt and the kids

alone. She had used herself as bait to lure the danger away from the others.

She cared so much about everyone…but herself.

"It took two of you to replace one of me," Zeke taunted him as he pushed Whit forward with the barrel of the gun buried between his shoulder blades. "You really think you alone are any match for me?"

"Are *you* alone?" Whit asked. He had seen no other men with the guard. And Zeke had been a helicopter pilot when he'd served his country and later when he'd served whatever country had paid him the most.

Zeke snorted. "More alone than you are. Where is she?"

"I told you. She's dead." He hated saying it; hated how the words felt in his mouth. Bitter and sickening. And he hoped like hell his superstition wouldn't be proved a reality. Ever.

"The next time I shoot, it won't be a coffee table," Zeke warned him. "And the only one who's going to be dead is you."

Whit chuckled and reminded Zeke, "But you're the one who's bleeding."

When the guard had shot the coffee table, Whit had struck him hard—trying to knock him out. But the man had an iron jaw. All Whit had done was broken his skin and drawn blood.

And rage.

Zeke had swung the gun toward Whit then. But he'd kept him from firing by saying that her body had washed up on the beach. And so he'd drawn Zeke outside to the steepest edge of the hilltop.

The wind picked up, and the pounding of helicopter blades alerted them to the arrival of another aircraft. Backup for Zeke?

But all his men must have been gone because he lifted his gun and aimed it at the helicopter. As it flew over them, Whit recognized the royal seal of St. Pierre. Maybe Aaron was inside—maybe he and Charlotte had figured out Zeke's duplicity and followed him here.

Zeke must have come to the same conclusion because he squeezed the trigger, getting off one shot before Whit struck him. Instead of swinging toward the man's iron jaw, though, he slammed his fist into Zeke's arm—with enough force to knock the weapon for his grasp.

The Glock flew from the man's hand, dropping over the cliff. While Zeke turned toward where it had fallen, Whit pushed—sending the man tumbling over the side.

But Zeke's arms thrashed. And as he reached

out, he caught Whit's shoulder and pulled him over the edge, too. He felt the weightlessness that he had when he and Gabby had jumped from the plane. But this time he had no parachute strapped to his back—nothing to break his fall on the rocks.

AARON'S HEART LURCHED as the helicopter took the hit. His gaze flew to the pilot, who grappled with the controls as the aircraft shuddered and shook. "This is why I wanted you to stay at the palace," he told his fiancée.

"And let you take on Zeke Rogers alone?" Charlotte asked, shaking her head at the thought.

"I would have brought some of the men Whit and I trust," he said.

She passed over the island, struggling to bring the helicopter under control again. Over open water, the engine sputtered once. Twice.

"We can't trust anyone," she said. "But each other…"

He trusted her. He trusted that if anyone could save them right now—it was her.

But what about Whit? Were they already too late to save him and Princess Gabriella? Were they on this island—as the parachuting and ocean current experts had told first Zeke and then them?

Or had they been lost at sea as Charlotte had been so convinced? She wouldn't let herself hope. Instead she'd been intent on tracking down who was responsible for the attempted kidnapping that had gone so very wrong...

And when they'd gotten on Zeke's trail, it had led them here. To this private island getaway. Or rather, hideaway, given that the man who owned it had used questionable methods accruing the wealth to acquire the island.

He could have been the one shooting at them. Whit wouldn't have been. He would have recognized the royal seal and waited to see who landed. Then he might have started firing if he'd realized Zeke Rogers had sold himself to a higher bidder.

Why had it taken the king so long to realize that Charlotte had been right not to trust the man? Why had he?

It was a mistake that had cost him. He'd aged another ten years with the realization that he had been the one who'd put his daughter at risk. Not Charlotte. Not Whit.

And what about Whit?

No bodyguard had ever taken an assignment as literally as Whit. He would do whatever was necessary to protect a client—even give up his own life for theirs. Aaron suspected that was never truer than now, with Princess Gabriella carrying Whit's child. The guy had always claimed that he would never get married, never be a father. Aaron didn't know his reasons why, but he doubted one of them had been death.

A dead man couldn't become a husband or father…

Aaron should have married Charlotte before they'd ever left Michigan. He shouldn't have let him talk her into making sure Gabby was safe first.

"That's definitely the helicopter Zeke took," Charlotte said. The royal seal was on the bottom of it but it was the same royal blue and bright magenta of the one she flew. Or tried to fly.

The engine sputtered again. They needed to land. But Zeke had planted his helicopter in the center of the small cement pad. The island wasn't big enough to have a clearing where they could land. There was only the house and then the hill dropped steeply off to the rocky beach below.

He trusted Charlotte. But there was only so much she could do. The helicopter was going down whether or not she found a place to land safely.

GABBY'S THROAT BURNED yet from the scream she'd uttered when she had watched the two men tumble over the cliff on the other side of the helicopter pad. She'd checked out the island earlier—when Whit was asleep. She knew this side had no stairs leading to a beach. It had no sand—only jagged rocks from the top of the hill to the water below.

Dread kept her legs locked in place—unable to move forward, to run toward the edge of that cliff. She had a horrible feeling that she knew what she would see when she looked over the edge.

Like a bird of prey, the helicopter circled back again. It was the colors of her country. But that offered Gabriella more fear than comfort. The only one she could trust who worked for St. Pierre was Whit.

And he was gone.

The helicopter engine sputtered. The metal screeched, trees scraping it, as the helicopter made its crash landing. It landed in a tiny clearing behind her, between her and the house. Leaving her an unobstructed view of that cliff.

She kept watching it. But Whit didn't pull himself up it. Neither did the man he'd pushed over the side. No one came back up.

Finally she forced herself to move toward where they had fallen. But her legs trembled so badly that she had no balance. She stumbled and pitched forward. To protect her baby, she put out her hands—and dropped the gun Whit had left her for protection into the thick grass.

Behind her the helicopter engine whined down to silence. It was eerily silent. So quiet that she heard the footsteps on the grass.

Panic overwhelmed her, sending her scrambling for the gun. She delved her hands into the grass. But it was so thick and long that she couldn't find the weapon.

She had nothing to protect her. No gun. No Whit. Tears of loss and fear and frustration stung her eyes, so that they watered. And her throat filled with emotion. She couldn't even scream.

But what did it matter? Who would hear her? Anyone who cared was gone.

Strong hands grasped her arms and pulled her to her feet. She drew in a shuddery breath, trying to summon the strength and courage to fight.

Whit might have been gone. But she still had her baby. She had to fight for him—to protect him and herself from whoever had come for her.

So when she turned, she lifted her leg and kicked out with her all might—hoping to knock her attacker's legs from beneath him—

hoping to knock him off balance enough that she could escape.

But there was more than one.

Chapter Thirteen

Aaron caught Charlotte, stopping her fall. Gabby gasped in shock over seeing her sister and realizing that she'd nearly knocked down the woman—the very pregnant woman.

"Oh, my God!" she exclaimed. "Are you all right?"

Charlotte nodded. "Are you?"

The tears she'd momentarily blinked away rushed back, filling her eyes and her throat, so she barely got out her, "Yes."

It had been Charlotte and Aaron on the helicopter. Charlotte and Aaron who had nearly crashed. She'd nearly lost them, too.

"Where's Whit?" Aaron asked anxiously, his blue eyes bright with fear for his friend's safety.

Hysteria threatened, but Gabby pushed it back to reply, "Whit's gone…"

"Where's Whit?" Aaron asked, glancing

around the small area. "Did Zeke take him somewhere?"

Zeke Rogers. That was who had landed in the first helicopter. That was who had fired those shots. That was whom Whit had been fighting when he went over.

"Come quick," Gabby ordered. She hadn't believed help would come, but it had. So maybe she needed to believe again—in Whit. To hope...

"They were fighting," she said, gesturing ahead of her at the cliff as she struggled to run through the tall grass, "and they fell."

She ran but Aaron wasn't pregnant, so he was faster. He beat the women to the cliff, stopping only at the edge. His jaw clenched as he stared over the side.

When Gabby rushed up, he turned around and stopped her with his arms on her shoulders. "Don't look!"

That had been her first instinct, too, not to look when she was so certain of what she would find. Utter despair and loss. But she hadn't thought there would be help, either. She hadn't really believed that anyone would ever find her and Whit. So she had to look. Had to know for certain...

She tugged free of Aaron's grasp and looked around him. Her gaze was immediately drawn to the edge of the water below, to the body so busted up on the rocks so that it looked like a broken marionette.

"That's not Whit," she said with horror. It couldn't be Whit. He couldn't be gone.

But they wouldn't be able to confirm or disprove the identity of the body because waves tugged at it, pulling it from the rocks to disappear into the ocean.

She screamed.

WHIT'S ARMS BURNED with his effort to hang on, his hands wrapped around a rock jutting from the cliff. The rock was damp, and his grip began to slip. He didn't want to wind up like Zeke, who'd crashed onto the rocks below. His eyes had been wide open, staring up at Whit in death. But now he was gone.

And Whit heard Gabby's scream. It chilled his blood with fear—for her safety more than his.

"Gabby!" he yelled back. "I'm coming. I'm coming!"

He wouldn't leave her—not like this. Not any way. As one hand slipped off a wet rock, he lurched up, reached out blindly with his free arm and somehow managed to clasp another rock while not letting go of the one he held. The rough edges cut into his palm, and his shoulder strained with the movement. But he didn't care. His own discomfort was nothing in comparison to the fear and anguish he'd just heard in Gabby's scream.

She screamed again—his name. But now her voice was full of hope and relief. "Whit!"

He stared up at the hilltop and found her leaning over the edge. A rock beneath her foot slipped loose and tumbled down the cliff. And she slipped, too.

"Gabby!"

But strong hands grasped her arms and pulled her back. He couldn't see her—couldn't see who had her or if she was really safe.

"Gabby!"

Now someone else stood on the edge, staring down. "Son of a bitch," a deep voice shouted. "What the hell…"

"Aaron!" Relief that Gabby was safe flooded Whit. His friend would protect her, like Whit had tried, with his life if necessary.

"How the hell am I supposed to reach you?" Aaron asked with frustration, as if he were trying to figure out a particularly vexing puzzle.

Whit's grip, on one rock, slipped again. But once again he held tight with the hand that had a hold on a rock and swung his free arm. He managed to catch the edge of another rock—higher up. "I'm coming," he assured them.

Aaron must have taken him at his word because he disappeared from sight. Disappointment and panic flashed through Whit. They had only just regained their friendship and their trust. So he suffered a moment's doubt—wondering if his old friend was really going to help him.

That panic had him swinging his arm again, trying to reach a higher rock. But his fingertips slipped off, and his arm swung back—nearly making him lose the grip he had with his other hand. He kicked out, trying to find a toe hold.

And beneath him the waves crashed against the rocks, as if getting ready to carry his broken body out to sea, too.

But he wasn't giving up. Not yet. Not ever. He swung his arm toward the wall of rocks again—trying to catch hold. And his fingers touched something else—rough fibers. A rope dangled over the edge.

"Grab it!" Aaron shouted.

Whit grasped the rope in a tight fist. But he didn't let go of the rock with his other hand. And finally he got a hold with his foot.

"I got you," Aaron said. "I can pull you up."

Maybe he could. While not as big as Whit, Aaron was a strong guy. But still Whit couldn't completely give up control or trust. Instead of just holding on and letting Aaron pull him up, he used the rope as a railing to make the climb himself.

He was climbing up to Gabby—to make sure she was safe. Even though Zeke was gone, it wasn't over. If Zeke had been working for someone, that person could hire another mercenary to finish the job. But even if they figured out whom Zeke had been working for, Gabby would always be in danger; her life and her safety always at risk because of who she was. Princess Gabriella St. Pierre.

And he was just a royal bodyguard…with nothing to offer her but his protection. And he hadn't done a very damn good job of protecting her yet.

She would be safer with Charlotte. And happier with a prince. So when he stepped foot on the topside of the hill, he resisted the urge to grab her up in his arms and hold her close. And when she reached for him, he caught her hands and stopped her from embracing him. Because if he gave in to temptation and hugged her, he would never let her go again.

"Are you all right?" she asked, her beautiful face stained with tears she'd shed over him.

She was too good for him. Too good for anyone…

"What the hell happened?" Aaron asked.

Whit nodded. "I'm fine. It was Zeke who hit the rocks."

Charlotte nodded. "We figured it was Zeke."

"Acting out of revenge," Aaron said, "for us getting him fired."

Whit shook his head. "It was about money."

"Was he going to kidnap me to get my father to pay him a ransom?" Gabby asked. She tugged her hands free of Whit's, as if self-conscious that she'd reached for him and he'd held her off. She slid her palms over her stomach, as if to soothe their baby.

He could walk away from her—to keep her safe. But could he walk away from his son? Hell, the child—heir to a country—would probably be in even more danger than Gabriella had been.

"I think it was about money," Whit agreed. "But I think someone was paying him…"

Gabby flinched, as if in pain. And he couldn't add to that—couldn't tell her what Zeke had been paid to do: kill her.

"You're not feeling well," he said.

She glanced up at his face, as if dazed. And she began to tremble. "I'm fine," she said. But she had to be lying.

"Aaron, get them back to St. Pierre," he ordered.

"What about you?" Aaron asked. "Aren't you coming with us?"

"I need to clean up around here—make sure Zeke was alone." And that the man was dead. He intended to go down to the beach below.

And Charlotte and Aaron must have read his intentions. "Aaron can stay with you. I'll take her," the former U.S. Marshal said. "We have a pilot with us."

"But your helicopter was hit."

"The bullet did no structural damage."

"Is the pilot someone we can trust?" Whit asked. Before they could answer, he shook his head. "You better fly them, Aaron." Because somewhere out there, someone still wanted Gabriella dead.

"I'm the one who flew us here," Charlotte said. And then she was the one who'd landed the helicopter after it had been hit. "I've had my pilot's license for years."

"Of course you have," Gabby murmured— with a flash of bitterness.

And Whit remembered that the women had unfinished business between them. Charlotte had kept secrets from Gabby that she'd had no right to keep even though she'd had her reasons. Maybe sending the two of them off alone together wasn't the greatest idea.

"So let's go," Gabby said, and she left him without a backward glance—as if she'd dismissed him after he'd done his job. Was that all he was to her? An employee? While she walked away, Charlotte and Aaron embraced—as if the thought of spending just mere hours apart was intolerable to them.

"Be safe," Aaron implored his fiancée.

"Always."

"I love you."

"I love you more," she said and pressed a hand to her own swollen belly. "Because I love you for the both of us." With another quick kiss for her baby's father, she followed Gabby to the helicopter pad.

Both men stood until the helicopter lifted off and flew away—its engine loud and strong and its course straight.

"No smart remarks?" Aaron asked.

"About what?" He knew, though. He'd teased Aaron in the past about his public displays of affection. The man always fell easily and hard. But he'd never fallen as hard as he had for Charlotte Green, and those feelings were so much stronger because they were reciprocated. Whit couldn't tease him about that—not when he was envious as hell of what his friend had found.

Aaron narrowed his eyes, which were an eerie pale blue, and studied Whit's face. "Are you really okay? You didn't hit your head when you went over the cliff?"

Whit shook his head. "There are steps over here leading down. We need to check down there—"

"He's gone," Aaron said. "There's no way he survived that fall." He shuddered. "I can't believe that you did—that you caught yourself. You are so damn lucky—like a cat with nine lives."

Whit nearly shuddered, too, at Aaron making the same comparison the mercenary had.

"But knowing you like I do, you probably used up the last of those nine lives today," Aaron continued. "So we shouldn't risk going down that cliff."

"Maybe Zeke lost his phone," Like he'd lost his life, on the rocks, "when he fell. If we can find that and figure out who he was talking to, maybe we can figure out who hired him."

"You think Gabby's still in danger?" Aaron asked, with a glance toward the sky—obviously concerned about both women. But the helicopter was long gone.

"I know she is." And even after they found whoever had hired Zeke, she would still be in danger—still have people trying to kidnap her for her father's fortune.

"What else do you know about her?" Aaron asked. "Who the father of her baby is?" The question was obviously rhetorical; his friend was pretty damn sure it was his.

Whit clenched his jaw.

And Aaron whistled. "I can't believe it—after everything you've said about never getting married—"

"That hasn't changed," Whit said. There was no way in hell a princess would ever consider marrying him. And even if she did take the chance on him, her father would never approve their marriage.

"And the fact that we have a job to do hasn't changed, either," he continued. "We need to protect her."

"From whom, do you think?" Aaron asked.

Whit shrugged. "I don't know. We thought it might be Prince Linus's father. She doesn't think her ex-fiancé could have concocted that elaborate a plot on his own."

Aaron gasped. "King Demetrios and his younger son are at the palace. They said they were concerned about her. Why would they want to hurt the princess?"

Whit shook his head. He couldn't fathom why anyone would want to hurt Gabby. "I don't know if they're involved. All we know for certain is that someone wanted her to *never* return to St. Pierre."

And Gabriella was already on her way…

"I DON'T NEED to ask who the father of your baby is," Charlotte remarked, once she and Gabby walked into their private suite of rooms in the palace.

They hadn't talked at all on the helicopter. Gabby hadn't been ready to deal with the woman she now knew was her sister. Nor had she been able to deal with her disappointment over how Whit had treated her. It was like their making love had been just her dreaming.

Because he had acted like it had never happened. He had acted like they had never been intimate enough to have conceived the child she carried. His child.

"You don't?" Gabriella wondered. Because Whit had certainly not betrayed their relationship. But Charlotte had always been able to read her—even while she, herself, had been keeping so much from Gabby.

"You love Whit," Charlotte said, her voice soft with sympathy. From the way he'd acted, she had undoubtedly been able to tell that Gabby's feelings were not reciprocated. "You were falling for him six months ago, but now you love him."

Gabriella shrugged. It didn't matter how she felt since her feelings were not returned. He'd asked her to take a risk on him...

A risk that he would figure out how to love? That risk had obviously not paid off.

"I don't need to ask who the father of your baby is, either," Gabby said, her heart warming as she studied Charlotte's face—so like her own except for the happiness that illuminated it from within—making her breathtakingly beautiful.

"I got pregnant the night of the ball," Charlotte said, pressing her palms to her belly as Gabby always did. "The same night I assume you must have since we both left the next day." Her light of happiness dimmed. "I'm sorry. I'm sorry that my plan went so wrong."

"You were the one who was kidnapped," Gabby reminded her. "I'm sorry..."

Charlotte shook her head. "It wasn't your fault. None of it was. Aaron found me." The light inside her brightened again. "He rescued me."

"He loves you."

Charlotte smiled. "Yes. He asked me to marry him, and I accepted. I love him."

Gabby flinched with jealousy and then was angry with herself for being so petty as to envy someone else's happiness.

Charlotte reached out, pulling Gabriella into a close embrace—or as close as their pregnant bellies allowed. "And I love you," Charlotte said. "That's why I couldn't tell you that I'm your sister. I couldn't tell you about our mother."

"But you knew how the queen hated me," Gabby said, pulling free of her. "You knew how that bothered me." Even after the woman had died. "You could have told me she wasn't really my mother."

Charlotte shook her head. "If I told you the truth, I would have been fired. It killed me to keep it from you, but it was better to keep the secrets and keep you safe."

Whit had been right about her reasons. Tears stung Gabby's eyes. "You—you wanted to tell me?"

Charlotte nodded, and the gesture had tears spilling from her eyes to trail down her face. "As soon as I found out I had a sister, I wanted a relationship with you. That's why, when I found the letter in the things my mom left behind when she died, I quit the U.S. Marshals."

"I thought you quit because of what happened with Josie and Aaron and Whit."

Charlotte had had Whit help her fake Josie's death so that she could relocate her. Making Whit keep the secret from Aaron had destroyed their business partnership and their friendship.

"Making Whit keep that secret…" Charlotte let out a shuddery breath. "I understood what it cost him…when I had to keep secrets from you."

"It won't cost you what it cost Whit," Gabby assured her. "You won't lose me." She hugged Charlotte tightly. So tightly that their babies kicked in unison.

Charlotte laughed. "They're already getting to know each other."

"They're going to be close," Gabby said.

"And so are we now that we have no secrets." Charlotte squeezed her. "Thank you for forgiving me."

"It wasn't your fault," Gabby said. "It was his…" Her stomach churned as she thought of him and how little he'd really thought of her.

"He apologized to me," Charlotte said. "He wants to treat me as a daughter now. Not an employee. Aaron will continue to work for him and protect us all."

What about Whit? But only Whit could answer that.

"He wants to make up the past to me," Charlotte said. "And I'm going to stay here and give him the chance."

Her sister was more forgiving than she was.

"He wants to see you," Charlotte said.

To control and manipulate her, no doubt.

She shook her head, wanting to put off the moment when she had to face her father, and all his disappointment. "I need to get ready first."

"Sure, clean up."

She didn't need a shower. She needed to gather all her courage and resentment and tell her father that she was not one of his loyal subjects. She was his daughter, and he was finally going to treat her and her wishes with respect.

"Don't keep him waiting too long," Charlotte said. "He's been through a lot these past six months. Thinking you were dead…" Her voice cracked with emotion as she added, "…and that I was dead, really changed him."

"He's not going to fire you over my finding out that you're my sister?"

Charlotte shook her head. "No. He acknowledged me as his daughter."

Maybe that was because he was about to disown Gabriella for letting him worry for six months and for getting pregnant with the baby of a man who wasn't royalty—except for being a royal bodyguard.

Whit had risked his own life to protect Gabby. But before she could romanticize his actions, she had to remind herself that he'd only been doing his job. She meant nothing to him.

"I'm glad I'm not the only princess now," Gabriella said. "But be careful that he doesn't try to run your life as he has mine."

"Talk to him," Charlotte urged.

Was it possible to talk to someone who had never listened to her? She nodded, acknowledging that she had to at least try.

Charlotte smiled as she headed for the door. "I'll let him know that you'll be meeting with him soon."

As soon as she could gather her courage and control her anger over all the secrets he'd kept from her. To splash some water on her face, Gabby stepped into her bathroom and gasped in shock.

Scrawled across her mirror in scarlet red lipstick was a note even more ominous than the letter left under her pillow. "You should have stayed dead!"

Chapter Fourteen

"I want to see her now!" Prince Tonio Malamatos commanded Whit as he paced the front salon of the palace. It was the most public parlor, the one farthest from the royal quarters and the royals.

Whit's head was still pounding from his struggle with Zeke Rogers. But he wasn't above fighting another man, and this tall thin man would be easily beaten. If only Whit had that right...

Gabby carrying his child wasn't enough—not when she was still engaged to this man. An engagement he apparently had every intention of seeing through to his wedding day—even though his ex-fiancée had arrived at the palace with him. Damn Aaron for hurrying off to find Charlotte as soon as they arrived, leaving Whit alone to deal with this royal pain in the ass.

He wasn't the only one demanding to see

her. King Demetrios had also requested an audience with her, to extend his apologies for the behavior of his son, and, Whit suspected, to introduce her to his other son. The young man followed his father like a puppy, like the ex-fiancée followed Prince Malamatos. Whit had had other men follow them back to their rooms. Men he trusted stood guard to make sure they wouldn't leave their rooms undetected.

"She needs to rest and recover," Whit told the prince. "She's been through a lot."

King Demetrios had accepted that excuse the first time Whit had offered it, and he and his son had retired to the guest rooms King St. Pierre had offered them. Prince Malamatos was much more stubborn.

"Whose fault is that?" the woman asked, her tone as waspish as her thin face. Honora Del Cachon, with her pale face framed with thin, dark hair, was a brittle and bitter woman—some distant relative of the queen. The queen had already been dead when Whit started working for the king, so he'd never met her. But meeting this woman gave him some indication of what Gabby had dealt with, and how she'd grown up with disapproval and resentment and cruelty.

Whit was hurting too much and too tired

to worry about protocol. Hell, he didn't remember what she was anyways—a princess? A duchess? He figured she was just a royal bitch. "I could give you a list of names of men who were trying to hurt her."

But still one name eluded him. He and Aaron had found nothing of Zeke's—not even his body. While they'd been searching the island, they had had the guards they trusted searching Zeke's apartment. They had found nothing there to indicate who had hired him—if anyone even had. There had been nothing to link him to anyone else. Maybe he had been acting on his own—out of vengeance.

"You are not going to take any responsibility for the princess's condition?" the woman demanded, her tone as imperious as the king's.

She was not a queen; Whit knew that much about her. Obviously she did not realize that herself. And how the hell did she know that Gabby was pregnant?

Aaron had said that only he, Charlotte and, *damn it,* the king knew.

"What do you mean?" he asked her.

"Are you not a royal guard?" the woman said. "Is it not your duty to protect her?"

"I am her fiancé," Prince Malamatos declared. "I will protect her from now on."

"She's been hiding for six months," the

woman said, turning now on the man to whom she'd been engaged. "She does not want to marry you."

"She was frightened," the prince stubbornly defended Gabriella. "I will hire many royal guards, men who can be trusted, and she will feel safe in my palace."

"She is pregnant," the woman said, betraying that she did know a secret.

Prince Malamatos didn't react to her news; obviously it wasn't news to him. Who had already told him? This woman or Zeke Rogers?

"How do you know?" Whit asked her.

The woman's shoulders lifted in slight shrug. "I saw her and the one who looks just like her as they arrived," the woman explained. She leaned closer to Whit, as if ashamed that she was about to gossip. "They are both the king's daughters, you know. The queen, my dear cousin, revealed to me on her deathbed that they are both his children by a former mistress. He bought her Gabriella like one would buy a doll or a puppy."

The prince betrayed no surprise. Obviously he already knew that, too.

"Why are you really here?" he found himself asking the man. Did he want to marry Gabby or punish her for betraying him during their engagement? St. Pierre wasn't that far away in geography or culture from the places that practiced honor killings. Was Prince Malamatos's country such a place?

"That's impertinent of you," the prince replied. "But as I told you, I want to see my fiancée. I want to set a date for our wedding."

"You still want to marry her?" the woman asked. "Even though she is pregnant with another man's child." From the arch glance she cast at Whit, it was apparent she knew which man.

The prince shrugged. "To merge my country with the resources of St. Pierre, I will claim the royal bastard as my own. After all, I will be marrying a royal bastard."

Whit wasn't tired enough to ignore what the man said. Or maybe he was too tired to summon the control it would have taken him to ignore that comment. For he swung and smashed his fist into the prince's weak jaw.

The man crumpled to the ground, the woman screaming and hovering over him.

"Whit!" Aaron yelled as he walked back into the salon. "What the hell!"

"Did you hear what he said about the princess?" Whit demanded.

"It was all true," the woman replied. "You are a barbarian."

He was a man in love. But all he could offer

Gabriella was his protection, of her life and her reputation…

"The king wants to see you," Aaron told Whit.

Whit's stomach knotted with dread at the look on his friend's face. He couldn't meet his gaze. Obviously the king was furious with him. Someone must have told him about the baby.

"He's going to fire you for your impudence," the woman said.

If he was going to get fired for it, he might as well tell the king exactly what he thought of him and the way he'd treated the sweetest woman Whit had ever known. He stormed past Aaron, heading toward the king's private rooms.

GABBY ROSE UP on tiptoe and tried to scrub at the mirror with a tissue. She scrubbed so hard that the mirror actually cracked from the pressure she applied—and probably from age, as well. It was an antique with a gilded frame.

Perhaps she should have called Charlotte back and shown her the message on the mirror. But Gabriella had chosen to ignore it—at first. She'd showered and changed into a gown. Since it was evening, formal dress was protocol even if there hadn't been guests in the palace. Fortunately she'd found a dress with an empire waist and a skirt billowy enough for her pregnant belly. Wearing a tiara was also protocol, so she'd turned to the mirror in order to see where to pin the diamond-encrusted jewelry into her hair.

And she hadn't been able to ignore the message any longer. Because the shower steam had smeared the lipstick and sent it running down the glass in rivulets, Gabby couldn't see beyond it.

And she wasn't certain she wanted Charlotte to see it. The last time she'd shown her a threat, her bodyguard had whisked her away and they'd both disappeared for six months. Gabby wouldn't have minded going back to the orphanage, but she couldn't now that people knew she'd been there.

Was there any place for her to be safe? She thought of Whit's arms, wrapped tight around her, her head on his chest with his heart beating strong and steady beneath her ear. She would be safe with him—only with him.

The door creaked open, and she lifted her gaze to the mirror to see who'd come up behind her. Her heart filled with hope that it was Whit—that he was back and had come to see her the moment they had landed.

It was probably Charlotte though, prodding

her because she'd kept the king waiting too long. Keeping him waiting was never wise. But then she peered around the lipstick blocking the image in the mirror and realized that he would probably be waiting longer.

"Hello, Honora…" She turned to greet the woman holding a gun on her.

"You are not surprised to see me."

She gestured behind herself at the mirror. "I figured out that was your shade. It certainly isn't mine."

"Of course not," Honora snapped. "You wouldn't wear something so stylish."

"I was thinking…" Garish. But it wasn't wise to provoke the lunatic holding a gun on her. "…exactly that."

"You've always envied me," Honora said.

"I have…" Given her very little thought over the years. The queen's cousin had always been unpleasant to Gabby—even when they were children.

"You've always wanted what I have."

A nasty disposition? Dissatisfaction with everything in life? Hardly.

"That's why," Honora continued, "you had your father arrange your engagement to my fiancé. You have to have everything I have."

For years Gabriella had just thought her cousin was nasty; she hadn't realized that the woman was actually delusional and paranoid and possibly mentally ill. "I'm sorry..."

"You should be—you will be—for trying to ruin my life!" Honora raised the gun so that the barrel pointed at Gabby's heart.

"I'm sorry that my father manipulated all of us," Gabby said. "It was him. Not me. I didn't ask him to break my engagement to Prince Linus."

"You would have married that psychopath?"

She shouldn't throw stones, but Gabby wasn't about to offer her that advice. "I had no idea my father was going to arrange an engagement with Prince Malamatos."

"Of course you did," Honora scoffed. "Of course you put him up to it. And of course your father will give you whatever you want. He has spoiled you rotten, just as my cousin the queen complained."

Gabriella snorted in disgust. "The queen constantly complained."

"Do you blame her?" Honora asked, obviously outraged on her dead relative's behalf. "She was forced to raise her husband's bastard as her own. That was cruel."

No, how the queen had treated Gabriella had been cruel. She hadn't cared that she'd been an innocent child, unaware of her parents' duplicity.

"As cruel as it will be if you were to try to force Tonio to raise your bastard as his own."

"I wouldn't do that," Gabriella insisted.

"You won't have to," Honora said. "Tonio is an honorable man. He intends to claim your bastard, which is more than I can say for that barbarian that actually fathered your kid."

"Barbarian?"

"The American," she said, her lip nearly curling with disdain. "The golden-haired one. I can understand why you would bed him…" She gave a lusty sigh. "But you should have been more careful than to become pregnant with his child. But then, of course, your father was careless too when he got his mistress pregnant with first your sister and then you."

Apparently Gabriella had been the only one not privy to the secrets of her family. She pressed her palms to her belly in which her child moved restlessly. "I don't regret this baby."

"I regret you," Honora said. "I wished you had never been born. So I will fix that now." Her finger twitched along the trigger.

"You don't want to kill me," Gabby bluffed. "You just don't want me to marry Prince Tonio. And since I have no intention of doing that, there is no reason to hurt me." Or her child.

Honora chuckled bitterly. "You would be a

fool to break that engagement. Not only is he a handsome, powerful man but he is the only one who'd be willing to marry a woman carrying someone else's bastard."

"I don't want to marry anyone," Gabby insisted. She wanted to punch this woman in the face for the horrible name she kept calling her baby. She drew in a deep breath and reminded herself that Honora was sick.

"You're lying!"

She expelled the shuddery breath she'd just drawn. "Yes. I am."

The gun trembled in Honora's hand. "I knew you were lying. I knew you wanted Tonio—because he's mine!"

"He is yours—all yours," Gabby assured the deranged woman. "I don't want to marry *him*. But I do want to marry someone."

The woman stared at her through eyes narrowed with skepticism and faint curiosity. "Who do you want to marry?"

Gabby stroked her hands over her belly, and she couldn't stop her lips from curving into a wistful smile. "The father of my baby."

But Whit marrying her was about as likely as Gabriella being able to talk Honora out of shooting her. She had to try…getting through to Honora. She'd given up on Whit. He'd faced death dangling from a cliff, and even that close scrape hadn't lowered his guard enough for him to let his feelings out. Maybe he really didn't have any feelings—for her or anyone else.

"THAT BARBARIAN?" Honora scoffed. "He has nothing to offer you."

Whit couldn't argue with her—even if he dared let his presence be known to either woman.

He had been on his way to see Gabriella and say goodbye when he'd noticed that royal bitch slipping into Gabby's private rooms. His first thought had been to turn around and leave without saying goodbye. But then he'd noticed the glint of light off the metal object Honora gripped in her hand.

A knife? A gun?

She wasn't sneaking into Gabby's room for girl talk. For revenge for her broken engagement? Was she the one who'd paid Zeke to make sure Gabriella never returned to St. Pierre?

He slipped into the room behind her. But before he could grab her, she'd pulled the gun. If only it had been a knife…

He could have pulled his trigger and killed her before she got close to Gabby. But with the gun, even if he shot her, she might reflexively pull the trigger. She might kill Gabby—or the baby—even as she was dying.

"Whitaker Howell," Gabriella saying his name drew his attention back to her, "is twice the man that Tonio Malamatos is. I don't want your prince, Honora."

The woman gasped in shock and horror. "Do you really expect me to believe that you would prefer a bodyguard over a man who will soon rule his own country and, according to the deal he made with your father, this country, as well?"

If Malamatos thought King St. Pierre was about to step down as ruler of the country named for him, he had gravely misunderstood their deal. Or was that just the reason he'd given his crazy fiancée for breaking their engagement?

Maybe old Tonio had been afraid of telling the woman the truth—that he just didn't want to marry her. Whit opened his mouth to draw the woman's attention to him and away from Gabriella.

But then Gabby was speaking again. "Whit Howell is a hero," she said. "He was a hero during his deployments with the U.S. Marines, and he was a hero protecting his clients. And he saved my life more than once."

"Zeke Rogers assured me that no one would,"

Honora said. "I paid him a lot of money to make sure you would never return to St. Pierre."

"He died trying to do the job you hired him to do," Gabby said—with apparent sympathy for a man who'd intended to kill her.

How could she be that selfless? That good? Especially given how no one had ever given her the love and concern that she freely offered to everyone else. She was just innately good. More people like her were needed in the world—not fewer.

Honora shrugged off any responsibility. "Your barbarian killed him."

Zeke's death had been an accident. Whit had wanted him alive, so that he would be able to tell them who had hired him. But he'd pushed him too hard...

"Whit is not a barbarian," Gabriella said. "He's a good man."

How could she say that about him? How could she see in him what he had only seen in her?

"You really are in love with a bodyguard," Honora remarked as if horrified.

"Yes," Gabriella said—as if proud of the declaration.

Could she actually love him?

No. She was probably just trying to convince the crazy lady that she was no threat to her relationship with the prince. Gabriella St. Pierre was far smarter than anyone had given her credit for being—including this jilted fiancée.

"Then you're stupider than people think," the woman replied. "Your father will never approve. In fact he just fired the man."

Gabby gasped now. "He fired Whit?"

The woman uttered a cackle of pure glee. "Guess he didn't approve of the hired help getting his daughter pregnant."

King St. Pierre hadn't actually explained his reasons for terminating Whit's employment. He'd just bellowed that he was done here and had only hours to leave the palace and St. Pierre.

Honora was probably right that the man had wanted better for his daughter than a bodyguard. And he wasn't wrong. Her other fiancés had been able to offer her palaces and countries. Whit didn't even have a home to call his own.

Never had...

That was why he hadn't argued with King St. Pierre. He'd only nodded in acceptance and walked out. He'd figured it was for the best— for Gabriella and for their baby.

Whit couldn't give them what the prince

could. But he could give them what the prince couldn't: his protection. He lifted his gun.

But he had to get Gabriella's attention to let her know that she would need to get out of the way when bullets started flying. She needed to drop to the marble floor or jump into the marble tub. He had to make sure that neither she nor their baby was hit.

But Honora was still talking, still taunting Gabby with knowledge she must have gained from spreading money around to servants or from listening at doors herself. "And Howell packed his bags and left without ever bothering to come say goodbye."

"That's not true," he corrected the woman. "I came to say goodbye. But you first, Honora…" Hoping that the woman turned toward him, with her weapon, his finger twitched on the trigger.

He had to make this shot count. Had to kill her before she killed Gabby. And he had to make damn sure he didn't miss and kill the woman he loved himself.

Chapter Fifteen

"Stop!" Gabriella yelled but not at the woman who held the gun on her. "Don't shoot her!"

She had only just noticed Whit when, with his gun drawn, he'd stepped through her bathroom doorway. So she had no idea how long he had been standing there.

Long enough to realize that Honora was mentally ill?

Long enough to learn that Gabriella was hopelessly in love with him?

Whit held his fire—probably out of instinct more than his actually caring what she'd said. "You tell me to shoot on an airplane but not in your bathroom. Afraid I'll break the mirror and get seven years of bad luck?"

The mirror was already broken—the bad luck all hers. Or maybe not.

Honora swung toward him with her gun drawn.

"Don't shoot him, either," Gabriella said. "You don't want to kill him."

"Because you love him?"

"Yes," Gabriella said. "And because he's an amazing shot. He will kill you, and then you will never have a future with Prince Tonio."

"I have no future with him now!" Honora trembled with rage. But instead of firing at Whit, she turned back to Gabby. "Because of you!"

Gabby shook her head—as a signal for Whit, and Charlotte and Aaron who'd snuck into the room behind him, not to shoot Honora. "I don't want to marry your fiancé," she reiterated. "The only man I will ever marry is the man I love."

And that was what she had intended to tell her father when she met with him. Now she may never get the chance to talk to him.

"All I want is to marry the man I love," Honora said. The facade on her thin face cracked like the mirror behind Gabriella. "But he doesn't love me…" She lifted the gun again, but this time she pressed the barrel of it to her own temple.

"Don't!" Gabriella said. "Don't do it!"

Honora's finger trembled against the trigger as her whole body shook. "Why not? I have nothing to live for."

"What you feel isn't real love—real love is reciprocated."

Gabby needed to remind herself of that—

that what she felt for Whit wasn't real. It wasn't what Aaron and Charlotte had. She may have gotten pregnant the same night Charlotte had, but that was all their situations had in common.

While the woman appeared to contemplate Gabby's declaration, she was distracted enough that Whit reached out and snapped the gun out of her hand.

"Noooo…" Honora cried, and she crumpled into a ball on the floor.

Gabriella reached out and touched her hair; it was as brittle as the woman herself. "You'll be okay," she said. "We'll get you some help. It'll get better."

"I'm sorry," she said, her voice breaking with sobs. "So sorry…"

"Get her help," Gabby told the others.

"I'm not leaving you alone with her," Whit said, stepping closer as if he intended to step between them.

But Honora was no threat. With her arms wrapped tight around herself, she was barely holding herself together.

Outwardly Gabriella probably appeared calm. But inside, she was shaking as badly as her would-be killer. She realized she'd taken a risk in not letting Whit just shoot the woman.

But too many people had already died. She hadn't wanted anyone else to lose their life.

And although she and her baby had escaped harm, she was shaken at how close a call she'd had.

"I'll stay while you get help," Charlotte offered. "I'll make sure they're both okay." She looked at Gabby as if she knew that nerves and emotions swirled tempestuously beneath the surface. And she knew that Gabby needed Whit gone so that she wouldn't fall apart and fall at his feet, begging him to love her back.

"You need to talk to the king anyway," Aaron told Whit.

Had Honora been telling the truth? Had he been fired? And was he going to just leave without saying whatever he must have come here to say to her?

He walked out without a backward glance. And Gabriella's heart cracked like the mirror.

"I FIRED YOU," King St. Pierre reminded Whit of their conversation only an hour ago. "Then I told Aaron to make sure you had left my property. Instead he found you saving my daughter's life."

"She saved her own life." Because if he'd shot Honora as he nearly had, she might have fired, too. And if a bullet had struck Gabby or the baby...

The king's brow furrowed, as if he tried to fathom how the princess could have protected herself. "Did she use the maneuvers her sister taught her?"

So he really was claiming his oldest as his daughter, too, now.

"No, Gabby used her innate talent—the one no one taught her," Whit said and with a pointed stare at the king added, "and the one no one managed to destroy."

Anger flashed in Rafael St. Pierre's dark eyes. "What do you mean?"

"No matter how cruel your wife was to her or how disinterested you were, she never grew bitter or selfish," Whit said, amazed at the strength that had taken Gabriella, even as a child, to remain true to herself. "She stayed sweet and caring, and it was those qualities that saved her life. She talked Honora out of hurting her and out of hurting herself."

The king sucked in a breath of surprise. "Gabriella did that—on her own?"

Whit nodded. "Despite my interference, she calmed Honora down." He flinched as he remembered how the woman had reacted to his presence. Maybe if he'd stayed quiet, if he'd trusted Gabby to take care of herself, she would have reached the woman even sooner.

The king uttered a heavy sigh of regret. "Are you sure it was Honora who paid Zeke Rogers to kill Gabriella?"

"She confessed to all of it." Actually she had bragged about it, but he suspected now that that bravado was part of her illness.

Gabby had been right to save her. The woman could be helped, and he knew his sweet princess would make sure she got help.

The king stared at Whit. "You may need to testify to what you heard."

He nodded. "Fine." He wanted the woman put someplace where she couldn't hurt herself or anyone else again.

"So you will need to remain on St. Pierre until her trial."

"I thought you wanted me out of your country," Whit reminded him now.

"Perhaps I reacted before I had time to understand the situation."

The fact that Whit had gotten his daughter pregnant while she was engaged to another man, a man who was now really free and ready to commit to someone else—was that the situation the king had needed time to understand?

Whit needed more time because he still

didn't understand it, had no idea why Gabriella would even look at him much less let him touch her. Make love to her...

He had nothing to offer her. Nothing like her other fiancés. But maybe he had something...

Maybe he had the one thing no one else had ever given her...

"You have my permission to explain yourself," the king said, as if issuing a royal decree.

"You're not the one I need to explain myself to," Whit said, only just realizing himself what he had to say and to whom.

The king's face flushed with fury as he slammed his fist onto his desk. "If you intend to continue in my employ, you will damn well answer to me."

The fist pounding didn't intimidate Whit in the least. In fact it amused him how a grown man could act so like a spoiled child. "You already fired me."

"That was precipitous of me. If you explain yourself, I will reinstate you," the king said, offering another royal decree.

And Whit chose to ignore this one, too. "I'm not going to tell you what you want to hear," he said, "so you might as well fire me again. Or still."

"Young man—"

"You know what—it doesn't matter if you've fired me or not," he said. "I can't work for you any longer. I quit."

"What the hell are you doing?" Aaron asked the minute Whit slammed open the door and stalked into the hall. He must have nearly knocked his old friend over with the door, for Aaron had jumped back. "You can't just walk away from this job."

"I can't work for him." It didn't matter what King St. Pierre thought of Whit and what he had to offer his daughter. It mattered more to Whit what the king had never offered Gabby—his love or respect. And he couldn't work for a man so stupid and cruel.

"Why not?" Aaron asked. "You two are awfully alike. And I do mean awfully."

If he wasn't so damn tired—physically and emotionally—Whit might have swung his fist into the other man's face for uttering such an insult. "I am nothing like that man."

"You're both stubborn and selfish and think you're always right and you appoint yourself to decide what's right for other people."

Whit flinched at the anger and resentment in his friend's voice. Aaron might as well have physically struck him because the hit was that direct. And probably that accurate.

Maybe he'd been a fool to think that Aaron

could ever forgive him, that their friendship could ever be repaired after Whit had betrayed him.

"I thought you were done being mad at me."

"I am," Aaron said. "But if you leave here, *she* will never get over being mad at you."

"Gabriella?" Whit chuckled. "She just forgave the woman who tried to have her killed."

"Honora may have threatened her, but she never really hurt her," Aaron explained. "You've hurt her. I saw it on that cliff—when you wouldn't let her hug you. And I saw it in her rooms when you turned and walked away—like you're walking now."

He was actually tempted to run as he headed toward his room in the employee's wing. This time he would finally pack up his things. There was nothing for him here.

"I can't believe you're being so stupid," Aaron said, following him like a dog nipping at his heels. "You already know how hard it was to find a job like this but you just willingly gave it up."

"There are other jobs," he said. "Hell, I could re-enlist if I can't find anything else."

Aaron sucked in a breath of shock. "You'd go back to active duty?"

"Why not?"

"I can give you two reasons—Gabby and your baby," Aaron said. "You might be able to find another job, but you'll never find another woman who loves you like she does."

He had never found anyone who loved him at all—let alone like Gabby had claimed to love him. "She was just saying those things to Honora," he insisted, "to make the woman think she was no threat. To make her think she has no intention of marrying Prince Malamatos."

"You think she does intend to marry him?" Aaron asked.

He shrugged. "As his ex-fiancée said, the man's quite a catch. A real prince of a guy."

"She's crazy," Aaron reminded him, "and so are you if you walk away from a woman like Gabriella."

"You've thought me crazy before," Whit said with a shrug, as if his friend's opinion didn't matter. But it mattered a lot—especially that Aaron believed she loved him.

But then Aaron had never been the best judge of character—because, like Gabby, he always saw the best in everyone. Even Whit.

Conversely, Whit always saw the worst in everyone—even himself. Except for Gabby— because there was only good in her.

And if he was the man she and Aaron thought he was, he would walk away and give her a chance at the life she deserved—that she had been born to live.

"YOU FIRED the man who saved my life!" Gabby accused her father the moment she stepped inside his rooms.

His shoulders drooping, he sat behind the desk in his darkly paneled den. His hands cradled his head, as if he had a headache or was trying hard to figure something out. Veins popped on the back of his hands and stood out on his forehead. He looked stressed and weary, as if he'd aged years in the six months she and Charlotte had been gone.

Despite her anger and resentment with him, affection warmed her heart. No matter how he had treated her and those she cared about, he was her father and she loved him. She nearly opened her mouth to tell him so, but then he lifted his gaze.

Instead of looking at her face, he looked at her belly—at the child she carried. And she thought she glimpsed disappointment on his face.

That was all she had ever done with him and the queen. Disappoint them.

"Whitaker Howell quit," her father corrected her.

She shook her head. "I heard that you fired him."

"Perhaps," he admitted with a slight nod of acquiescence, "but then I gave him the chance to stay, and he chose to leave."

Of course he chose to leave. Now that she was safe, he had no reason to stay. He had done his job. And that was all she must have been to him.

She blew out a ragged breath of pain and regret that he hadn't tried to stay, that he hadn't at least tried to love her and their baby.

Take a risk on me...

She had risked everything—her heart, her future, her baby's future. And she'd lost him.

"But Prince Malamatos is here," the king continued. "He refuses to leave until he sees you and makes certain you have survived your ordeal."

"Ordeal?" she asked. "I hope you're talking about recent events and not the six most useful and productive months of my life."

"At the orphanage?" he asked, with a brow raised in skepticism. "I can't believe Charlotte sent you there to hide."

"I'm glad she did," Gabby said. "Otherwise I might have never learned the truth."

The king's mouth drew into a tight line of disapproval. Had he never intended to tell her the truth?

"I was referring to the country she sent you to," he clarified, "and how dangerous it is."

"Yet I was in no danger until everyone learned where I was." And then because she had to know, she asked him, "Would you have ever told me?"

"About your mother?" he asked and then uttered a heavy sigh. "I promised the queen that I would never..."

Because then Gabriella might have realized that it hadn't been her fault the woman hadn't loved her... The woman had been cruel right up until the end. "After she died, you could have told me."

He sighed again. "But your biological mother had already died, so there seemed no point in dredging up ancient history."

And probably his embarrassment over his affair with a con artist.

"No point in my getting to know my sister and my aunt?" Perhaps he hadn't wanted her to get to know and emulate two of the strongest women she had ever met—because then she wouldn't blindly obey him. His efforts to keep her ignorant had been futile. It didn't matter how short a time Gabriella had known them;

she was still going to emulate them. He was done controlling her life.

"We will discuss this another time," the king imperiously announced—which meant that he never intended to discuss it.

Because he had been wrong and would not admit it. And he compounded that arrogance when he continued, "You have kept your fiancé waiting long enough."

She shook her head. "Prince Malamatos is not my fiancé. He's yours. You chose him. You can marry him. I'm not."

"Gabriella!" The king shot up from his chair, anger turning his face a mottled red. "You are impudent."

"No," she said. "But I should have been before now. I should have made it clear to you that while you rule this country, you do not rule my life. I will make my own decisions from now on."

He pointed to her belly. "Being a single mother is what you choose?"

No. But she couldn't force the baby's father to love her. Too weary to deal with her father, she turned toward the door.

"Prince Malamatos will claim the baby."

"Like the queen claimed me?" she asked. "I won't take the risk of his treating my baby the way I was." She wanted to give this child two parents who loved him. And Honora had already shared Tonio's opinion of Gabby's baby; it was an inconvenience but he would adjust to include it in his plan of ruling two countries.

"You need to talk to your fiancé," he persisted, "and let him discuss your future."

Another man telling her what to do? Disrespecting what she wanted?

She shook her head. "No one talked to me about this engagement. You didn't. Tonio didn't. I don't even know the man. Why would I even consider marrying him?"

"You have always been so naive and idealistic, Gabriella, believing in fairy tales of love and happily-ever-after," her father said with a snort of disdain. "That is why I have had to make your decisions for you."

She turned back to him and met his gaze and decided to share with him the real struggle between them. "I want to hate you, Father."

He sucked in a breath, as if she had struck him in the stomach. Or perhaps the heart…

"But I can't," she assured him. "I feel too sorry for you."

Pride lifted his chin. "You feel sorry for *me?*"

She gave him a slight smile, one full of pity for all he had missed experiencing. "Because you have never been in love."

"What makes you think that?" he asked, but he didn't rush to deny her allegation either.

"Because if you had ever felt love—true love—yourself," she explained, "you would not try to force me to marry someone I don't love…"

He studied her face as if he were truly seeing her, as if he had really heard what she'd told him. Perhaps it was a first for them. Then he cleared his throat and asked, "You love Whitaker Howell?"

"Yes."

He dropped heavily back into his chair. "He did not stay," he said, as if warning her. "He did not fight for your hand in marriage."

She flinched as if he'd struck her now. And he had aimed directly for her heart. "It doesn't matter whether he stays or goes." It did not change the fact that she loved him. That her heart would belong to him and no other—certainly not any fiancé her father found her.

The king chuckled. "You were never able to lie. I could always tell whenever you tried to be less than truthful with me."

"If only I had been able to tell the same," she murmured. It would have saved her from all the years she'd spent in the dark, oblivious to all his secrets and lies.

He heard her. His skin flushed again. But he

ignored her comment and continued, "You are lying now. Whether Whitaker Howell stays or leaves, it matters to you. Greatly."

She shrugged. "But *I* don't matter to him. Even you said that he wouldn't fight for me."

"He fought for you," the king reminded her. "He fought to save your life. He fought to find you these past six months."

"He was just doing his job," she told him, as she'd kept telling herself.

The king shook his head. "Not just his job. He cannot say enough good things about your caring and your selflessness."

"He can't?" Hope flickered, warming her heart.

The king grinned and nodded. "He loves you."

Gabby's head pounded with confusion. "Then why would he leave?"

"Because you are a princess and he is a bodyguard. He thinks he has nothing to offer you." The king's brief grin faded. "And he's right."

"If he loves me," she corrected her father, "he has *everything* to offer me." Because love was all she had ever wanted...

She turned toward the door. But her father made a sound, something akin to a sniffle, that had her turning back to him. He lifted his gaze to hers, and his eyes were wet with emotion. "I have loved you," he said, as if he'd read her mind, "I have always loved you."

She had waited her entire life for her father to declare his feelings for her. But suddenly how he felt didn't matter so much to her anymore. "I have always loved you, too," she said. It was why she had always tried so hard to please him. But now she wanted to please herself. So she headed for the door.

"He's probably already gone," her father warned her.

Probably. But she would not be deterred now. "Then I will find him."

"It took us six months to find you," he said. "It'll take you much longer to find Whitaker Howell if he doesn't want to be found."

Chapter Sixteen

"Stop!"

The shout reverberated off the walls of the corridor leading away from the wing of employees' rooms. Just as he had earlier, Whit automatically obeyed. He froze in place, his suitcase clutched in his hand.

"That's the second time today that you've told me to stop," he said, turning toward her.

Gabriella's eyes were bright with anger—an anger so intense that she trembled with it. She wasn't the only angry one.

He kept flashing back to what had happened with Honora, and in his head, it ended differently—it ended badly, with Gabriella bleeding on the floor. "You could have gotten yourself killed the first time."

"She wasn't going to hurt me," Gabby insisted.

He dropped the suitcase, so he could reach out and shake some sense into her. But he only closed his hands around her bare shoulders. Then he had to fight the urge to pull her closer. And never let her go…

But first he had to deal with other emotions—with the helplessness and fear that had raged through him when he'd stood in the doorway watching that madwoman threaten the mother of his unborn baby—the woman he loved.

"She hired Zeke and those other men to kill you," he reminded her. "She didn't intend to just hurt you—she intended to kill you!"

"She intended for them to kill me," she agreed—maddeningly. "Them—not her. She isn't capable of personally killing someone—it made it real for her. And she realized that it was wrong."

He tightened his grip on her shoulders, tempted again to shake her. She was so sweet and innocent, so hopeful that there was goodness in everyone. "Murder is wrong no matter if you do it yourself or hire someone else to do it for you."

"She's not well," Gabby defended the woman who'd nearly killed her.

"And neither are you," he said, "for taking the risk you did with yourself and our baby."

"Our baby?" she asked, her eyes widening with shock. "You're claiming him now?"

He narrowed his eyes at her. "I already have. I never doubted that he was mine."

She narrowed her eyes back at him. "Not for a moment? Not even when you met Dr. Dominic?"

"I hate that guy," he admitted, barely resisting the urge to grind his teeth with the jealousy that shot through him. He had never been jealous before—had never cared enough to be jealous of anyone else.

Her lips curved into a slight smile. "Of course," she agreed. "He moved to a third-world country to offer his services free to take care of orphaned children. He's a horrible, horrible person."

A grin tugged at Whit's lips, but he fought it. He knew how ridiculous he was being. "Yes, a horrible person."

"And ugly, too," Gabby said, her brown eyes warming and twinkling as she teased him back.

His heart pounded harder with excitement; the woman attracted him more strongly than any other woman ever had.

"I'm glad you see that, too," he said.

"I always thought he was hideous," she said with a girlish giggle.

"A regular Dr. Jekyll and Mr. Hyde," Whit added.

Her amused smile faded. "No. That would be you."

He chuckled at the illogical insult. "How's that?"

"One minute you're this sweet, funny guy and the next you're acting like my father," she accused him, "bossing me around and unilaterally making decisions that affect both of us."

"What decisions have I made?" he asked. She and Aaron had both really read him wrong. But then it wasn't their fault when he'd been afraid to make himself clear before now.

She pointed a trembling finger at the suitcase. "You decided to quit. To just take off and leave me and your baby behind without another thought."

He chuckled at how wrong she was. "You're more like your father than I am," he argued. "You're the one who keeps shouting out orders at me."

"Is that why you quit?" she asked. "You're sick of getting bossed around?"

Aaron had already told him he was a damn

fool for quitting. But Whit didn't want to do this as her father's bodyguard—as a member of the staff or even as the baby's father.

"By your father, yes," Whit agreed. "But I think I'm getting used to your bossing me around."

He slid his hands from her shoulders, down her bare arms to grasp her hands. Once their fingers were entwined, he dropped to his knees. "And just so you know…I could never not think about you. For the past six months every thought I had was about you."

She sucked in a sharp breath, pulled her hands free of his, and touched her belly.

"Are you okay?" he asked. "You're not having contractions or anything?"

She bit her lip.

He pressed his hands over hers on their baby. "Gabby, are you all right?"

She nodded. "I just…" Her voice cracked with the tears that pooled in her eyes. "I can't believe this… I thought you were leaving. Or that you might already be gone. And I didn't know if I could find you…if my father was right and you didn't want to be found…"

She was chattering as nervously as she did for reporters until Whit reached up and pressed a finger across her lips. "Shhh…"

She stared down at him, her eyes so wide with fear and hopefulness.

"I had no intention of leaving without you," he said, still on his knees. "I know you never wanted to come back here. That's why I quit. I didn't want to force you to live where you've never been happy."

Now the tears fell with such intensity she trembled as uncontrollably as she had when they'd been freezing in the sea. "I will be happy wherever you are."

"So you'll marry me?"

She threw her arms around his neck and clung to him, too choked with sobs to answer him.

Was she saying yes? Or sorry? He couldn't understand her. "Gabriella?"

She loved him; he knew it. But was love enough to overcome their differences?

"You haven't answered me," Whit said, his voice gruff with impatience as he closed the door to her suite behind them.

"I will answer your question," she said, "after you answer mine."

"What question can you have?" he asked. "I thought my proposing said everything."

Of course he did. He was a man. He didn't

understand that she needed more of an explanation. That she needed more...

"Why did you propose?" she asked, her heart beating frantically with equal parts hope and dread. "You haven't told me yet *why* you proposed." But she had a horrible suspicion she knew the reason, that she carried it in her belly.

His brow furrowed with confusion. "I thought my reason was obvious."

She touched her belly. The baby moved restlessly inside her. "I hope it isn't..."

His mouth dropped open with shock, and then his jaw tightened and a muscle twitched in his cheek. He was obviously offended and angry. "You think the only reason I want to marry you is because you're pregnant?"

That was her fear—that he only wanted her for what she was—the mother of his child—and not for who she was.

Too choked with fear to answer him, she simply nodded.

He chuckled. "You and I are quite the pair, aren't we?"

"What do you mean?"

"I would have told you how I felt earlier," he said, "but I didn't think you could love me."

Shock and sympathy for the pain that flashed

across his handsome face had her gasping. "Why not?"

His broad shoulders lifted and dropped in a heavy shrug. "I didn't think I had anything to offer you."

"Didn't you hear what I told Honora about you?" she asked, pretty certain that he had been there at least long enough to have over-heard some of what she'd told the deranged woman. "About all the reasons I love you?"

He nodded. "I heard, but I thought you were lying—that you were tricking her into think-ing that you didn't want her fiancé."

"You thought it was all a ploy? Everything I said to her?" Was it that he thought that lit-tle of himself or that much of her? "You think I'm that smart?"

"I know you're that smart," he said. "And you're loving and caring and forgiving. You're so damn beautiful inside and out that I couldn't even believe you were real. I thought you were just some fairy-tale princess until that night…"

Her face got hot with embarrassment. She had been unbelievably bold that night. He had tried to be all business—just a royal body-guard. But she had undressed in front of him…

"I'm talking about earlier that night," he said, as if he'd read her mind. Maybe he had noticed that all her skin had flushed with desire and her pulse was leaping in her throat. "About when you got so angry you actually pounded on me."

She laughed. "You like abuse?"

"I like everything about you. Your sweetness and your fire. Your patience and your passion…"

"Like?" she asked. "I need more to say yes." She needed love.

"I love you with all my heart," he said. "That's the only reason I want to marry you." He laid his hand on her belly. "This baby is just a bonus—like the prize in a box of Cracker Jack."

"Cracker Jack?"

"I forget that you're not American," he said. "Cracker Jacks are—"

"I know what Cracker Jacks are." She wrinkled her nose at his less than romantic compliment. "Sticky popcorn."

"Sweet." He leaned down and brushed his mouth across hers. "And I love sweets…"

"And I love you," she said. She lifted his hand from her stomach to her arm and then she squeezed his fingers together. "Pinch me to prove this isn't just a dream."

He moved his hand from her arm to her butt and pinched.

She squealed—with shock and delight. Then she reached around and pinched his butt.

He laughed out loud. "I can't believe this is real, either," he said. "You make me happier than I thought it was possible to feel. You make me *feel*."

And so many people had warned her that he couldn't—that the man didn't have a heart. But as his arms closed around her, she laid her head on his chest and heard his heart beating strong and fast. For her...

His hands cupped her face and tipped it up for his kiss. His lips brushed across hers. But then he deepened the kiss. His tongue slid inside her mouth, tasting and teasing her.

Gabby didn't want to be teased anymore. She wanted to make love to the man she loved. So she unbuttoned his shirt and unclasped his belt. Whit helped her discard his clothes. Then he reached for her and the zipper at the back of her gown. He fumbled with the tab before tugging it down. Her dress slid down her body—leaving her naked but for a bra that barely covered her full breasts and a thin strip of satin.

He did away with her underwear, too, and then—despite her extra weight, he easily lifted and carried her to the bed. "You are even more beautiful now than you were that night," he said, his hands stroking over her more generous curves.

"I'm huge," she said, pursing her lips into a pout.

He kissed her mouth. "You're beautiful." He kissed her cheek. "Breathtaking…" He kissed her neck.

She moaned as desire quickened her pulse so that it raced. And her skin tingled.

"You're beautiful," she said.

With his shock of blond hair and dark eyes, he was beautiful—and strong with muscles rippling in his arms and chest. And his back.

She dug her fingers in, clutching him close. "I am so in love with you." She had fallen for him at first sight and then she had fallen harder and deeper the more she'd gotten to know him. "You are an amazing man."

He touched her intimately, stroking her until she writhed beneath him. Pressure wound tightly inside her, making her body beg for release.

He lowered his head and kissed her breasts, tugging one nipple between his lips. He nipped gently at it.

And she came, screaming his name.

The man gave her pleasure so easily—so generously. She pushed him back onto the mattress and reciprocated. Her lips moved from his mouth, down his throat, over his chest. And lower. She loved him with her mouth, until he tangled his fingers in her hair and gently pulled her away.

"You're killing me," he said, his chest rising and falling as he struggled to catch his breath. "I can't take any more."

"You're going to have to get used to it," she warned him. Because she intended to spend the rest of her life loving him.

Whit couldn't believe how happy he was—how happy Gabriella made him. He wrapped his arms around her, holding her close as he rolled her onto her back.

She arched her hips. "Make love to me," she said, bossing him again.

And he loved it.

He groaned, his arms shaking as he braced himself on the bed and gently pushed himself inside her. But she tensed and gripped his shoulders.

"Stop!"

Sweat beaded on his upper lip, as he struggled for control. It reminded him of that night they had first made love—when he had discovered that she had never made love to another man before him. She hadn't told him to stop that night, though. She'd begged him to continue—to make love to her. And then she'd moved beneath him, taking him deep inside her.

"Why do I have to stop now?" he asked, gritting his teeth with the effort to control his desires. "Is the baby all right?"

"The baby is fine," she assured him. "But you shouldn't be."

"I'm damn well not fine," he said. "I want to make love to my fiancée."

"I am not your fiancée yet. I didn't answer your question," she reminded him. "I asked you why you asked. But I never answered you."

He tensed. "You told me you loved me, too." But she had never told him yes.

"But I haven't accepted."

"Why not?" Had she changed her mind? Did she think that love wasn't enough to overcome their different upbringings?

"I didn't have the chance yet," she said with a teasing smile.

The woman infuriated him and fascinated and captivated him.

"So what is your answer to my proposal?" he asked. "Will you marry me?"

"Of course I will marry you," she said, as if he'd been silly to worry. "I can't wait to be your wife."

He breathed a ragged sigh of relief. "And I can't wait to be your husband."

"Now," she said, "make love to your fiancée."

He chuckled. "You are getting really comfortable bossing me around."

She smiled. "Do you mind?"

He thrust gently inside her. "We want the same things," he said.

"Each other…" She moaned and arched, taking him deep inside her, as she raked her nails lightly down his back. She met his every thrust, moving in perfect rhythm with him.

She came, her body squeezing him tightly as pleasure rippled through her. And her pleasure begot his. The pressure that had built inside him exploded as he came.

"Gabriella!" His throat burned from shouting her name. He dropped onto his back next to her and wrapped his arm around her, holding her close to his side. "Now that I've made love to my fiancée, I can't wait to make love to my wife. We need to get married as soon as possible."

Then he needed to find a job and a house— someplace safe enough for him to protect a princess and a royal heir.

"I want to get married here," she said.

He sighed, hating that he was already unable to give her what she wanted. "I don't think your father will agree to that."

"I think he will," she said, "and I think he'd like you back working for him."

"I don't care what he wants," Whit said. After the way he'd treated his daughter, the man deserved little consideration for his feelings. But then Whit remembered how much the man had emotionally and physically suffered the past six months. "I care what you want. And you don't want to live here. You didn't even want to come back here."

"I didn't want to come back and marry a strange prince," she explained. "But I don't mind living here. No matter how much time I spent in boarding schools growing up, this was still my home."

"I never had a real home," he admitted.

"You do," she said. "With me and our baby."

"We're a family," he said. "But we need a home—one where I can keep you both safe."

"I think that home should be here," she said, "with Aaron and Charlotte and even my father..." She looked up at him, as if she held her breath waiting for his decision.

He could keep his wife and child safe here—especially with Aaron and Charlotte's help. "Are you sure this is what you want?"

She smiled. "Our baby growing up with Aaron and Charlotte's?"

"They're staying here?"

"Charlotte wants to get to know the king as her father. He asked her to stay—not as employee but as his daughter. I want to live with my sister. I want my baby to know his aunt and cousin."

She painted a pretty picture for Whit—not just of a home but of an extended family, as well.

"They say it takes a village to raise a child," he remarked.

"We have a country."

He grinned. "We have more than I ever believed I would have...because of you."

"We have happily-ever-after," she said. "Like a real fairy tale."

"And I have my real fairy-tale princess."

It was a dream—one he never would have dared to dream—but it came true anyway. And his happy present and future made him think of his past and someone who'd had to give up her home and her family or lose her life.

He hoped she'd found a new home. A new family and the happiness he had.

CHARLOTTE WAS HAPPY—happier than she'd thought possible as she lay in her fiancé's arms, listening to his heart beat strong and steady beneath her cheek.

But one thing marred her happiness and kept her from sleeping peacefully...

A man had killed trying to find out where a witness was. Like Zeke Rogers, he'd been paid. They had found out who'd hired Zeke, but she had yet to find out who had hired her former partner to locate Josie Jessup.

No one but she, Aaron, Whit and Gabriella knew where JJ was. But it worried her that someone else out there knew the woman was alive and was determined to find her. And Charlotte didn't even dare try to contact Josie to warn her. Because whoever wanted to find her knew that Charlotte was the one who'd hidden her. They were undoubtedly waiting for her to lead them right to Josie.

And only the devil knew what they intended to do when they found her. Kill her?

* * * * *

LARGER-PRINT BOOKS!
GET 2 FREE LARGER-PRINT NOVELS PLUS
2 FREE GIFTS!

◆HARLEQUIN®

INTRIGUE®

BREATHTAKING ROMANTIC SUSPENSE

YES! Please send me 2 FREE LARGER-PRINT Harlequin Intrigue® novels and my 2 FREE gifts (gifts are worth about $10). After receiving them, if I don't wish to receive any more books, I can return the shipping statement marked "cancel." If I don't cancel, I will receive 6 brand-new novels every month and be billed just $5.24 per book in the U.S. or $5.99 per book in Canada. That's a saving of at least 13% off the cover price! It's quite a bargain! Shipping and handling is just 50¢ per book in the U.S. and 75¢ per book in Canada.* I understand that accepting the 2 free books and gifts places me under no obligation to buy anything. I can always return a shipment and cancel at any time. Even if I never buy another book, the two free books and gifts are mine to keep forever.

199/399 HDN FVQ7

Name	(PLEASE PRINT)

Address	Apt. #

City	State/Prov.	Zip/Postal Code

Signature (if under 18, a parent or guardian must sign)

Mail to the **Harlequin® Reader Service:**
IN U.S.A.: P.O. Box 1867, Buffalo, NY 14240-1867
IN CANADA: P.O. Box 609, Fort Erie, Ontario L2A 5X3

**Are you a subscriber to Harlequin Intrigue books
and want to receive the larger-print edition?
Call 1-800-873-8635 today or visit www.ReaderService.com.**

* Terms and prices subject to change without notice. Prices do not include applicable taxes. Sales tax applicable in N.Y. Canadian residents will be charged applicable taxes. Offer not valid in Quebec. This offer is limited to one order per household. Not valid for current subscribers to Harlequin Intrigue Larger-Print books. All orders subject to credit approval. Credit or debit balances in a customer's account(s) may be offset by any other outstanding balance owed by or to the customer. Please allow 4 to 6 weeks for delivery. Offer available while quantities last.

Your Privacy—The Harlequin® Reader Service is committed to protecting your privacy. Our Privacy Policy is available online at www.ReaderService.com or upon request from the Harlequin Reader Service.

We make a portion of our mailing list available to reputable third parties that offer products we believe may interest you. If you prefer that we not exchange your name with third parties, or if you wish to clarify or modify your communication preferences, please visit us at www.ReaderService.com/consumerschoice or write to us at Harlequin Reader Service Preference Service, P.O. Box 9062, Buffalo, NY 14269. Include your complete name and address.

HILP13

The series you love are now available in

LARGER PRINT!

The books are complete and unabridged—
printed in a larger type size to make it
easier on your eyes.

◆ **HARLEQUIN**
Romance

From the Heart, For the Heart

◆ **HARLEQUIN**
MEDICAL™
**Pulse-racing romance,
heart-racing medical drama**

◆ **HARLEQUIN**
INTRIGUE·
BREATHTAKING ROMANTIC SUSPENSE

◆ **HARLEQUIN**
Presents·

Seduction and Passion Guaranteed!

◆ **HARLEQUIN**
super romance·

Exciting, emotional, unexpected!

Try **LARGER PRINT** today!

Visit: www.ReaderService.com
Call: 1-800-873-8635

◆ **HARLEQUIN**®

A *Romance* FOR EVERY MOOD™

www.ReaderService.com

ReaderService.com

Manage your account online!

- Review your order history
- Manage your payments
- Update your address

> ### *We've designed the Harlequin® Reader Service website just for you.*

Enjoy all the features!

- Reader excerpts from any series
- Respond to mailings and special monthly offers
- Discover new series available to you
- Browse the Bonus Bucks catalog
- Share your feedback

Visit us at:

ReaderService.com

RS13

REQUEST YOUR FREE BOOKS!

2 FREE NOVELS
PLUS 2 FREE GIFTS!

WORLDWIDE LIBRARY®
MYSTERY™
Your Partner in Crime

YES! Please send me 2 FREE novels from the Worldwide Library® series and my 2 FREE gifts (gifts are worth about $10). After receiving them, if I don't wish to receive any more books, I can return the shipping statement marked "cancel." If I don't cancel, I will receive 4 brand-new novels every month and be billed just $5.24 per book in the U.S. or $6.24 per book in Canada. That's a savings of at least 34% off the cover price. It's quite a bargain! Shipping and handling is just 50¢ per book in the U.S. and 75¢ per book in Canada.* I understand that accepting the 2 free books and gifts places me under no obligation to buy anything. I can always return a shipment and cancel at any time. Even if I never buy another book, the two free books and gifts are mine to keep forever.

414/424 WDN FVUV

Name	(PLEASE PRINT)	

Address		Apt. #

City	State/Prov.	Zip/Postal Code

Signature (if under 18, a parent or guardian must sign)

Mail to the Harlequin® Reader Service:
IN U.S.A.: P.O. Box 1867, Buffalo, NY 14240-1867
IN CANADA: P.O. Box 609, Fort Erie, Ontario L2A 5X3

Want to try two free books from another line?
Call 1-800-873-8635 or visit www.ReaderService.com.

* Terms and prices subject to change without notice. Prices do not include applicable taxes. Sales tax applicable in N.Y. Canadian residents will be charged applicable taxes. Offer not valid in Quebec. This offer is limited to one order per household. Not valid for current subscribers to the Worldwide Library series. All orders subject to credit approval. Credit or debit balances in a customer's account(s) may be offset by any other outstanding balance owed by or to the customer. Please allow 4 to 6 weeks for delivery. Offer available while quantities last.

Your Privacy—The Harlequin® Reader Service is committed to protecting your privacy. Our Privacy Policy is available online at www.ReaderService.com or upon request from the Harlequin Reader Service.

We make a portion of our mailing list available to reputable third parties that offer products we believe may interest you. If you prefer that we not exchange your name with third parties, or if you wish to clarify or modify your communication preferences, please visit us at www.ReaderService.com/consumerschoice or write to us at Harlequin Reader Service Preference Service, P.O. Box 9062, Buffalo, NY 14269. Include your complete name and address.

WWLI3